INDIAN SUMMER

INDIAN SUMMER

by Kanai Mieko

TRANSLATED BY

TOMOKO AOYAMA & BARBARA HARTLEY

East Asia Program
Cornell University
Ithaca, New York 14853

The Cornell East Asia Series is published by the Cornell University East Asia Program *(distinct from Cornell University Press)*. We publish books on a variety of scholarly topics relating to East Asia as a service to the academic community and the general public. Standing Orders, which provide for automatic notification and invoicing of each title in the series upon publication, are accepted.

Address submission inquiries to CEAS Editorial Board, East Asia Program, Cornell University, 140 Uris Hall, Ithaca New York 14853-7601.

Number 155 in the Cornell East Asia Series.
New Japanese Horizon Series Editors:
Michiko Wilson/Gustav Heldt/Doug Merwin
Copyright English language translation ©2012 Tomoko Aoyama and Barbara Hartley.
All rights reserved.
ISSN: 1050-2955
ISBN: 978-1-933947-25-9 hardcover
ISBN: 978-1-933947-55-6 paperback
Library of Congress Control Number: 2012931578
25 24 22 22 21 20 19 18 17 16 15 14 13 12

To all the

Momokos and Hanakos

everywhere around the world

Contents

Introduction

Some books have been destined to be cherished by generations of readers around the world. They represent a wide variety of genres, including children's literature and popular literature, which are often but not necessarily counted as belonging to the classical canon. One genre that has provided numerous texts which have won the hearts and minds of readers, indeed whole groups and generations of women both young and old, is that of girls' literature. By "girls' literature" I mean not simply the new or the older "chick lit" or the juvenile fiction and romance targeted at female audiences but more widely any literature that has attracted the sustained interest of (and has often been produced by) "girls" (young women and their sympathizers). While some of this material remains too culturally specific to be suitable for export, many books belonging to this genre are shared in translation by readers around the world. The genre has its own canon: one thinks at once of *Little Women*, of *Anne of Green Gables*, or of *The Secret Garden*. But in spite of its wide readership it is a genre which has seldom been the object of attention of "mainstream" literary studies.[1] This is in spite of the fact that, interestingly, many works that occupy central positions of the world's literary canon—Jane Austen's novels, those of the Brontë sisters, and even perhaps *The Tale of Genji*—are at the same time surely canonical texts of "girls' literature." This association, however, has been neglected, erased, buried, or simply elided in conventional literary studies.

The work of the brilliant contemporary Japanese author Kanai Mieko, surprisingly, has so far remained largely inaccessible to non-Japanese speaking readers, with the exception of one volume of linked short stories and several other short pieces.[2] We have undertaken the translation of *Indian Summer* in the belief that it is important to redress this lacuna. Moreover, we believe that this is a novel which deserves to enter the global canon of girls' literature. *Indian Summer* was first serialized in a magazine called *Ensemble*, the public relations magazine of Kawai Music Education, from 1985 to 1987 and published in book form in 1988, the same year in which Yoshimoto Banana's *Kitchen* appeared. There are, however, some differences between the serialized version and the two book versions: a hardcover edition published in 1988 by Chūō Kōronsha and the pocket-sized paperback edition published in 1999 by Kawade Shobō Shinsha. (This translation uses the Kawade edition with both 1988 and 1999 "Afterword" by Kanai Mieko.) The lovely black-and-white illustrations by the author's sister Kanai Kumiko that appeared in the serialization, for instance, were reduced in size and number as the publication form changed. More importantly, in the book versions Kanai Mieko cleverly added extra pieces of writing to make the story even more innovative than the first version. It is not really a case of revision as such; rather it is the adding of extra voices and viewpoints. I will return to this later but first let me introduce the outline of the novel—without spoiling the reader's pleasure. (Or of course, if you prefer, you are most welcome to go directly to Kanai's text and return to this introduction later.)

Indian Summer is narrated by Momoko, who at the beginning of the novel is a nineteen-year-old university student living with her novelist aunt in Mejiro, Tokyo. There are some contemporary urban scenes: shopping and dining in up-market Ginza and fashionable Roppongi, as well as the frequenting of cinemas and cafes in student quarters such as Takadanobaba. During the two decades that have passed since the publication of the novel, certain cultural icons (such as some art house cinemas) have disappeared; nevertheless most of the features of the milieus remain very much relevant. The most important topos in this novel (and in fact in a series of others of Kanai Mieko) is Mejiro, which is situated between the two huge Tokyo districts of Shinjuku and Ikebukuro. If the reader is familiar with the locality of these and other suburbs and quarters of Tokyo, so much the better, though such knowledge is by no means essential. This is true of many other details in the novel; geo-cultural knowledge adds pleasure, but even without it there is more than enough to enjoy. In this sense this is a very open and welcoming text despite its numerous references to specific names, places, and cultural items.

Indian Summer is more about friendship than about romance, the latter appearing in this novel only in comic, parodic or satirical forms. It has no Mr. Darcy (or Wickham) but it does have many characters as eccentric as Lady Catherine De Bourgh and Mr. Collins. Some of these eccentrics, however, are quite lovable or, occasionally, even admirable. In the early part of the novel the reader is introduced to two of Momoko's strong allies—her aunt and Hanako, a new friend whom Momoko meets for the first time at university. Momoko's novelist aunt, who appears from the opening pages of the narrative, has many peculiar habits. However, these pale into insignificance in front of the highly individualistic Hanako, who joins the aunt and niece pair in the fourth chapter. Even the relatively ordinary characters in the novel—including Momoko herself—are clearly distinct individuals. It is not that heterosexual romance is repressed in the novel; it is merely that none of the protagonist trio Momoko, Hanako and Momoko's aunt, has any dream or illusion about romantic love or sex. Many of these characteristics—eccentricity, friendship between girls, and critical stance to heterosexual romance and gender expectations—are shared by both earlier and later girls' texts.[3]

Indian Summer is full of comedy, irony, sarcasm, and cutting sociocultural critiques, often to do with gender. There are also some highly original memorable descriptions such as Momoko with a hangover observing her body while in the bath, or riding a bicycle with her friend along a street in Mejiro to buy some beer. Readers familiar with Kanai's earlier works may be surprised by the total absence of the vividly disturbing imagery which frequently appears in stories such as "Rabbit" and "Rotting Meat." Neither is Momoko's narrative as overtly metafictional as some other Kanai texts. This by no means suggests that *Indian Summer* is simple and naïve. In fact one of the charms of this novel is its complexity and ambiguity presented in an accessible language and form. The complexity is due partly to the structure of the novel, which, as pointed out above, Kanai elaborated upon further between the appearance of serialized version and the first book form. Scattered through Momoko's first-person narrative are her aunt's essays and short stories, to which Momoko is privy as the first reader before these works are sent out to various magazines and publishers. Each of these manuscripts adds ironical dimensions to Momoko's primary narrative, and vice versa. Furthermore, there is a certain polyphony in Momoko's narrative itself. It often includes reported and remembered secondary (or tertiary) stories as well as conversations, usually with Hanako and/or Momoko's aunt. The effect for the reader is that of joining in the "girls' imagined community."[4]

Intertextuality is a strong feature of *Indian Summer*, although, as with the Tokyo topography, it is not vitally important that the reader recognize every layer or intertextual thread of this novel. It might be helpful, however, to offer here a few notes on some of the pieces "written by" Momoko's aunt. "Flower Tales," for instance, is a hilarious (and in a sense quite affectionate) parody of Yoshiya Nobuko's *Hana monogatari* (Flower Tales), which captivated girl readers for at least half a century after its publication in 1916. The term "Onēsama" (big sister) used by Kanai's adolescent girl protagonist to refer to and address honorifically a beautiful young woman, the flower motifs, fashion details—all these are familiar elements in classic girls' stories established by Yoshiya. If the reader is familiar with Yoshiya's text, she or he will appreciate not just the skillful imitation and pastiche here but the stunning transformation of these familiar elements. Even if unfamiliar with this specific text (untranslated), however, the reader will still recognize that "Flower Tales" is a parody of a girls' story and will enjoy, in particular, the comic incongruity between the characters, motifs, and relationships in this story-within-a-story and those in Momoko's primary narrative.

Readers interested in semiotics, narratology, intertextuality, and, generally, film and literary studies will certainly find this text a treasure house. There is even an essay on Barthes (again, presented as a piece written by Momoko's aunt, but recognizably Kanai to her devoted readers). But we must emphasize again that such knowledge is not essential; the text offers so many different kinds of pleasure and we simply leave it to the reader to decide how much to absorb in the course of one reading, and whether, afterwards, to come back to discover more and more and/or to delve deeper into some particular aspects of the text.

So we as translators hope that you will enjoy this novel as much as we do. And if you do, you will perhaps be eager to read its sequels. *Kanojo(tachi) ni tsuite watashi no shitte iru 2, 3 no kotogara* (Two or Three Things I Know about Her (and Her Friends), 2000) is told by Momoko ten years after *Indian Summer*. Momoko and others appear in some other volumes of the ever expanding "Mejiro" series,[5] each of which is, unlike the fate that befalls many (most?) other sequels of popular novels and films, just as entertaining and witty as *Indian Summer*, but contains further thematic, structural, and stylistic innovations. Unfortunately none of these other texts is yet available in

English translation. We recommend Kanai's original writing to readers of Japanese. Some might like to produce their own translation, sequels, parody, pastiche, film, manga—just as we often do with other favorite books of ours.

Tomoko Aoyama

NOTES

1. There are some exceptions, including a chapter entitled "Little Women: The American Myth," in Elaine Showalter's *Sister's Choice: Tradition and Change in American Women's Writing*.

2. The only book-length translation of Kanai's work available to date is *The Word Book*, trans. Paul McCarthy, Dalkey Archive, 2009.

Other translated short stories include:

"Platonic Love," trans. Amy Vladeck Heinrich, in Van C. Gesssel and Tomone Matsumoto, eds., *The Shōwa Anthology: Modern Japanese Short Stories*, Kodansha International, 1979, 375–82.

"Rabbits," trans. Phyllis Birnbaum, in Phyllis Birnbaum, ed., *Rabbits, Crabs, Etc.: Stories by Japanese Women*, University of Hawaii Press, 1982, 1–16.

"Rotting Meat," trans., Mary A. Knighton, in *Fiction International*, 29 (1996): 110–15.

"Tama," [part of the novel *Tama ya*] trans. Mark Jewel, *Japanese Literature Today*, 14 (Mar 1989): 5–12.

"Treading on Soft Earth," trans. Sarah Teasley, *TriQuarterly* 99 (Spring-Summer 1997): 7–27.

There are also two poems:

"The House of Madam Juju," trans. Christopher Drake, in Howard Hibbett, ed., *Contemporary Japanese Literature: An Anthology of Fiction, Film and Other Writing Since 1945*. New York: Alfred A. Knopf; Borzoi Books, 1977, 342–43.

"In the Town with Cat-Shaped Maze," in Kenneth Rexroth and Ikuko Atsumi, trans. and eds., *The Burning Heart: Women Poets of Japan*. New York: The Seabury Press, 1977, 129–31.

3. Takemoto Nobara's 2002 novel *Shimotsuma monogatari* (trans. *Kamikaze Girls*), for example, shares not only these characteristics but also the name of the protagonist, Momoko.

4. Honda Masuko, *Jogakusei no keifu*. Tokyo: Seidosha, 1990, 179.

5. *Kaiteki seikatsu kenkyū* (A Study of the Comfortable Life, 2006), for instance, includes two chapters narrated by Momoko, who, in her thirties, is still living in the same apartment in Mejiro.

INDIAN SUMMER

by Kanai Mieko

1

⁓

"Well," I said, "it looks like I'll be staying with my aunt."

Now, even though the girls in my class knew nothing about my mother's sister, it was clear that they were pretty envious, and not just because my aunt was a novelist—they really thought there'd be practical benefits to my staying with Auntie. But you have to remember that they weren't all that bright.

My friends at school obviously thought that, with a few exceptions, novelists have loads of money which made them imagine that there'd be all sorts of advantages to my new place and that great things would happen to me—like I'd live as a pampered rich girl wearing designer clothes and going to trendy places—and they also seemed to have decided that, because my aunt is famous, she'd live a life of luxury with lots of friends in the media and that I'd meet some nice man, or at least be introduced to some important people who'd maybe give me a job in television or the media. They even thought that I'd get to go along if my aunt went overseas, as some novelists often do. Of course, since none of these naïve girls had read anything by my aunt or had a clue about how she lived, you could perhaps understand their getting carried away; but, if you ask me— and I'm sure that Auntie would agree—their ideas were pretty stupid really.

I met my aunt for the first time in five years when I stayed at her place in Mejiro after I enrolled in a special summer holiday intensive program while I was doing an extra year's study, having failed my university entrance exams. This gave me a whole month to observe her "novelist's lifestyle," and so, unlike my misguided classmates, I was under no ill-informed illusions about Auntie.

I didn't want to stay with my aunt when it came time for me to go back to Tokyo to attend university and neither did she really want me there, but we were both worn down by my mother's constant nagging.

"That woman is dreadful. She's just a self-centered old *réac*," Auntie said when we talked together later, and though the "dreadful" and "self-centered" immediately made sense, my aunt could see I was confused by the term, "*réac*." "Haven't you heard that term before?" she asked. "No," I said. "It's short for *réactionnaire*," she explained, but I still looked blank. "You don't know the French word for reactionary?" my aunt said scornfully, unimpressed at my dimness. "Let's hope you at least know what words like 'reactionary' and 'conservative' mean in your own language!" she said condescendingly.

My aunt was certainly right, though not about being shocked by the fact that I had made it to university without knowing the meaning of the word "réactionnaire." But she was absolutely correct about my mother being so conservative, something that was painfully obvious from the reason my mother gave for letting me go to university in Tokyo even though I was a girl. My brother, Jun'ichi, is two years younger than I am. "When it's time for Jun'ichi to go up to Tokyo for university," my mother said, "the two of you can get a flat or apartment together. That way, you'll be able to look after him. But," she continued, "since you're a girl, until then, you'll have to stay either with your uncle in Suginami or your aunt in Mejiro." You don't need to be a flag-waving feminist to take offense at her logic, but it's no use talking things over with my mother because once she makes up her mind, that's it.

"If I can't live by myself, I might as well go and stay with Dad," I said, knowing the sort of response this would get from my mother who looked suitably tense. "You might be a nuisance," she said. "And anyway," she added, "Papa doesn't live by himself so you'd be in the way." I told my aunt all this as she checked how much wax she'd removed from her left ear with a tortoise-shell ear pick. "I don't really want to hear about that never-ending saga," she said, still prodding away at her ear, clearly without the least interest in our Freudian "family romance."

So that was the beginning of my new life as a student.

Last year my aunt complained constantly that the summer heat made her lethargic, and menopause, she said, didn't help either. Once, when I spent the night away from home on some very personal business, she made no comment and I'm not even really sure she noticed. I'd been expecting a big lecture and had crept in as quietly as I could so it was a relief to be let off, but I was also a bit taken aback at being so obviously ignored. She seemed to find it all too much of a bother.

Even though it was spring when I returned to Tokyo, my aunt was still sleeping and lying around the house all day, but this time she blamed menopause, mid-life depression, and "these balmy spring days that famously make everyone so sleepy." I'd read her novels and respected and admired her, and I'd been really eager to find out how she lived, but it was all a bit disappointing.

The house I was born in and grew up in, you see, was also the house where my aunt, who is my mother's younger sister, was born and raised. Although the family business was an inn that would usually have been taken over by the eldest son— my mother's younger brother—they adopted a bridegroom for my mother when my uncle decided not to do this, and my parents then ran the inn. And that was how my younger brother, Jun'ichi, and I came to spend our childhood in the room where my aunt had also grown up.

At the beginning of April my mother came with me to Tokyo to attend the various ceremonies for beginning students at the start of the academic year and also to help set up my things in the four-and-a-half-mat room my aunt used as a storeroom cum library. Although it was past lunch when we arrived, my aunt greeted us in the shabby flecked grey tracksuit that doubled as her pajamas. "The doorbell woke me," she said opening the door. "We're terribly sorry," my mother replied. "It's dreadful of us to barge in on you like this. You were probably up working all night." But her apologies sounded pretty insincere because if she'd really been sorry she wouldn't have been bringing her daughter to stay; what she actually meant was, "You're her aunt. It's your duty to look after her."

That night we ate out, and then, because Mother insisted that we have an early night, declaring energetically that we would need to get up at first light to begin organizing the things that needed doing for me to settle in, we only unpacked the bedding from the big zip-up futon bags that had been delivered with my other luggage and left the day before in the living-room that doubled as my aunt's study. At 11.30 that night the phone rang. It was for me.

"Who is it?" my mother asked my aunt as, with both right beside me, I took the call. "I'm not sure," my aunt replied. "Just a friend I think." I wasn't too happy with the caller and hung up as soon as I could. "Who was it?" my mother asked again insistently, this time turning to me. "What sort of friend calls at this time of the night, especially when you've just moved in? Who does something like that? Come on, tell me who it was!" I didn't see any point in answering so I didn't say anything. "Can't you see how inconvenient this is for your aunt?" my mother continued in the face of my silence, trying to make an ally of her younger sister and drawing herself up as she spoke so that she now sat on the futon in formal style, legs tucked primly beneath her. Brought into the argument like this, my aunt became a bit flustered. "It's no trouble," she said. "I'll get another line installed so we don't need to bother with each other's calls and that'll suit us both." "That's beside the point," my mother snapped tensely. "This is *not* about getting an extra phone line.

What I want to know is who was on that phone!" My mother's tone became increasingly shrill as her hysteria mounted until she became so angry that she couldn't get back to sleep.

And while I was certainly annoyed with my mother, I was absolutely furious with the useless boy who'd called. "Now that you're here in Tokyo we'll be able to meet more often," he had said. "There's lots of places to go. I thought about contacting you sooner but didn't want to interrupt your study for the entrance exam. Then, when I went back home for the holidays, I met a girl who was in your class. What's her name—you know, her family has the cake shop near the station. She gave me your address and phone number. Was that your aunt on the phone? She sounded pretty annoyed." The caller prattled on. "Okay," I said. "See you some time." I didn't waste words. "So, it's okay then if I call back?" he pressed, sounding pleased. "Sure," I said and hung up.

The next morning the crows woke me. "Miaow, miaow." I could hear a high-pitched sort of caw which at first I thought was one of those sea gulls that sound a bit like a cat, but since there shouldn't have been any gulls in that part of Tokyo I asked my aunt why the local crows made a mewing sound. "The crows here mimic the cats to tease them," she said with a straight face, but I'm not sure whether or not this is true.

Meanwhile, back in the kitchen my mother was preparing breakfast. "We have a very busy day," she said briskly, "because we need to get on with clearing away all these boxes." My aunt sat reading the paper, pretending not to hear, while I dreamed about my new life, entranced by the sensation of the warm and balmy spring breeze blowing gently across the down on my arms; but Mother was having none of that and hurried us both along to the table. And that's how my "fresh new morning" began.

2

～

Char-grilled miso beef with grilled green pepper,
shiitake mushrooms and thinly sliced onions
in sweet vinegar
Scallops in sweet soy sauce
Grilled sea urchin
Grated yam and raw egg
New potatoes with deep-fried tofu and snow peas
Steamed English spinach with crushed sesame seeds
Baby turnips marinated overnight in salty plum paste
Cucumber and white radish slices marinated in miso
Miso soup with baby bamboo and seaweed
Steamed rice
Kiwi fruit, grapefruit and strawberry fruit salad
with sherry

This was the breakfast menu. "All it needs is some sashimi and gourmet vegetable tempura and you could serve it up for dinner at the inn," my aunt said, looking astounded.

"We've got a big day ahead of us," my mother said defensively. "We need to eat well to keep up our stamina."

"But there's too much. If I eat all this now I'll just go straight back to sleep."

"You don't have to eat everything," said my mother.

"It's impossible to eat everything," replied my aunt. "We're not plowing fields, you know."

"I've already told you that you don't need to eat it all. What's the matter with you?" My mother berated her sister. "Can't you do a bit of physical work without complaining? We're only moving a few things around a room." The air between the two sisters was becoming quite tense.

"Auntie's just saying that you've given us a bit too much breakfast. It doesn't take that much 'physical work' to tidy a room a bit," I said, with the emphasis on "a bit."

I could see my aunt's point of view, because, after all, she hadn't exactly been all that excited at the thought of my coming to live with her, a point that was pretty much lost on my mother. As for the breakfast, even I couldn't believe how much food there was. While studying for my second round of entrance exams, I'd got into the habit of making myself a midnight snack—my parents ran an inn and in the hospitality business even quite small children tend to be left to do things by themselves—so I hardly ever had an appetite in the mornings, and my stomach baulked at the sight of this breakfast table groaning with the gourmet food that was meant to prepare us for our day of physical labor. "I'll never know how that woman gets on working with people when she can't even understand her own family," said my aunt after my mother left. I agreed totally but when I told Auntie that I'd heard that the Moriya Inn might be put on the market, she looked quite forlorn at the thought of the family business being sold.

After breakfast there was a huge amount of food left because my aunt and I only ate rice, miso soup and pickles with some grated yam, raw egg and grilled sea urchin, and said we'd leave the rest for lunch.

"Good. I was going to order something in. But this will be fine," my mother replied as she covered each plate with plastic wrap. "So there," she declared victoriously, "I haven't prepared too much after all."

Since I knew my aunt's morning routine after spending time with her the previous summer, it was no surprise to me that, after drinking her milk tea and smoking a cigarette, she brought her toothbrush from the bathroom and lay down on the sofa to read the paper and brush her teeth. But this appalled my mother who apparently didn't know about my aunt's habit of earnestly cleaning her teeth for ten minutes several times a day—and I don't mean ten minutes in total, I mean ten minutes every time.

There are plenty of people who find an obsession with looking after the body extremely annoying—even if it is something important like cleaning your teeth—and, of course, it just so happened that my mother was one of these people.

"What are you doing cleaning your teeth like that for so long?" Mother questioned her sister sharply. "It must be dreadful having all that toothpaste in your mouth."

"No, it's not," said my aunt through her toothbrush. "I don't use toothpaste."

"Does she always do this?" my mother asked, frowning at me and then turning back to her sister. "If you keep brushing so hard, you'll damage the inside of your mouth," she said.

"No, I won't."

"Of course you will."

"I do it gently. You only cause damage if you brush too hard."

"Are you sure about that?"

"Yes. Here, look. I can massage my gums with this rubber tip at the end of the handle."

"So you're telling me your gums are infected?"

"No, I'm actually protecting my gums against infection."

"And you think that works?"

"It's the only way to do it."

"Does it always take so long?"

"Yep."

"Aren't you overdoing it a bit?"

"I like it. It feels good."

"Massaging your gums, you mean?"

"I'm brushing my teeth, too."

"This is nonsense."

"No, it's not. I love brushing my teeth."

"But you hated it when you were little."

"I didn't know then."

"Didn't know what?"

"The fascination of brushing my teeth, of course. What else?"

"What are you talking about? What fascination? It's just routine personal hygiene. There's no fascination."

"Yes, there is. I find the act of brushing my teeth seductively fascinating," my aunt said.

Here we go again, I thought, having heard my aunt's theories on the fascination of cleaning one's teeth the last time I stayed with her. Mother was keen to cut the conversation short and start preparing my room and, even though she and I rarely joined forces, I supported her on this point as I wanted to stake a claim to a space for myself sooner rather than later. Nevertheless, my aunt insisted on telling us how she'd been seduced by the act of brushing her teeth.

"I really hate going to the dentist and if I don't have problems then I don't need to go. By the way," she said as if she had just remembered, "I wrote a short essay while you two were asleep last night and just have to slip out for a minute to the local stationery shop to fax it off."

Various Reflections on Dentists

About ten years ago, I had treatment for three problem teeth and finally rid myself of the toothache that had plagued me for some time. Occasionally since then, when I have been busy with work and haven't looked after my teeth properly, I have had some early signs of gum problems and, although this was probably related to age, I found it quite worrisome. So, whenever there was any indication of trouble, I would spend half an hour cleaning my teeth each evening before bed and, up until now, this has helped prevent anything serious developing.

My dislike of dentists must surely relate to my experiences as a child.

I still feel a wave of nausea when I remember the dentist who treated my teeth when I was young: the black leather chair that stood in the surgery, the headrest covered by a white cloth; the black machine beside the chair—I have no idea what it was called but, with its electric drill that bored away at my teeth, to me it was like a malevolent instrument of torture—so that just the thought of either the equipment or the dentist, who liked to scream and yell at the least provocation, makes me absolutely furious. Even now, merely walking past the surgery can make me so angry that I avoid the street whenever I go home to see my family because, although I've been to several dentists since, none has been so callous.

More than ten years ago the place where I lived was owned by a dentist and, since I had a problem with a throbbing tooth, I decided to pay him a visit. This dentist cum landlord, who was getting on in years, told me his practice didn't process health insurance claims and, as paying full price would have made any treatment rather expensive, he introduced me to another dentist in the neighborhood. I had missed the rent a couple of times so perhaps he was worried I wouldn't pay my bill or perhaps he was just too old to be bothered with patients and their teeth. Two or three years later, a few cracks appeared in the rendering on the outside wall of my apartment and the damp came through when it rained, so I asked the landlord if it could be fixed, expecting him to call a repairman; but, instead, the old dentist himself came shuffling along, trowel in hand, whereupon he proceeded to shock me by filling up the cracks with the same flesh colored putty he used in his surgery. By then, the practice had been taken over by a son who had been in the United States and once, when I went to pay the rent and was chatting with the old couple, a young man in golf attire, who was obviously the son, walked through the living room wearing white patent leather shoes with shiny metal buckles— in spite of the fact that it was a tatami room and that he should have only been in his socks. I thought that he must just have forsaken Japanese etiquette while in America, but, when I told this story to a woman in publishing who lived in the apartment complex, she had an even more amazing story about how one day, when she went to pay the rent, the son was outrageous enough to walk straight through the living room stark naked just out of the bath.

But let me get back to the second dentist my aging dentist-landlord introduced me to—who was equally ancient and whose surgery had the same kind of black leather chair and intimidating black apparatus I had seen in other dental surgeries except that, in this case, all the equipment was about the same age as the owner. Entering this early 1950s time-warp, where the dental chair held a child whose screams and crying were accompanied by the din of a radio with the volume on high, was such a terrifying experience that I decided just to paint my problem teeth with iodine, take some aspirin, and put up with the pain. As I set off for home, hand pressed against my aching face, pain shot through my cheek with every step and my face was so swollen that I looked like someone with the mumps. So when I came across a tidy-looking dental clinic along the way, I decided to go in. Although I explained how much pain I was in to the unsympathetic-looking middle-aged woman in a white uniform at the reception desk in the corner of the empty waiting room, she responded curtly, "We only take people with appointments. Today and tomorrow are booked up," she went on, "but I might be able to fit you in if you come back the day after tomorrow."

In the hippy era and the days of anti-Vietnam War protests, there were two lapel badges that had been popular with student demonstrators—both drawn with simple lines and circles, one smiling and one crying. Advertisements for this dental practice featuring these two faces, one on top of the other, were pasted on electricity poles around the area, except that a compress tied at the top of the head in the manner of a child with the mumps had been added around the chin of the crying face. This was a patient before seeing the dentist while the smiling face represented the relief of someone after receiving treatment. Unfortunately, since I had been refused treatment because I had no appointment, there would be no smiling face for me.

Next, I went to a new practice in the area where the dentist fitted me in between patients with scheduled appointments but, since by now my mouth was too swollen to do dental work, he just examined my teeth, prescribed a painkiller and antibiotics, and explained that when the swelling subsided he would let me know exactly what needed to be done. I was so happy that someone had helped me at last. Several days later I went back to discuss my x-ray results and treatment plan and, while I sipped the coffee the receptionist made, the dentist nonchalantly passed me a roughly written memo with the estimated total cost of my bill. How I regretted accepting that coffee because while he might have relieved the pain in my mouth, I thought in despair, the damage to my hip pocket would be equally painful. The dentist claimed I needed implants in various places around my mouth at a total cost equivalent to two hundred pages, before tax, of literary journal manuscript. This would take me four or five months to write and was well beyond what I could afford.

Finally I found another dentist who did root canal treatment on three teeth, extracted two teeth and replaced them with implants, and also taught me how to use a toothbrush effectively. Thankfully, the total cost amounted to only thirty pages of manuscript production.

The root canal treatment took time and I ended up going to the dentist every couple of days for a month or so. It was here that I first came across the magazine, *President*, and discovered a totally new world that I had no idea existed. I was fascinated by the survival strategy tales of the managerial classes and wondered if the magazine had been put there for the patients, or if it was something the dentist subscribed to himself.

Two or three years later, this young dentist returned to his hometown to open a practice and, since it was just at the time when newspapers and weekly magazines ran a series of articles on exorbitant dental consultation fees, it seemed to me that he was going back to the country because he was too conscientious and ethical to run a successful business in Tokyo. In any case, it was he who taught me how to use a toothbrush and I have never been to a dentist since. ☜

"Auntie, why don't you take a walk after you fax the manuscript," I suggested. "Mother and I can organize things here."

"I'd like to, but I can't." My aunt was adamant. "If I leave you two to shift my books from the storeroom into my bedroom I won't know where anything is later. By the way," she added, "any chance of another cup of tea?"

"You haven't changed since you were a child," my mother snorted. "Whenever you had something to do, you'd keep procrastinating and putting it off. Later on, you'd end up having to do it anyway. I remember how you could never finish a school project on time. You'd be messing about all over the place and then panic at the last minute." My mother then turned her attention to me. "And you're exactly the same. That's what you do, too."

My aunt feigned defective hearing, although she did blush a little, but then she said, "What I was trying to say is that the mouth is the only place inside the body that we can actually wash, although I suppose you can wash your anus or vagina if you want to stick your finger in or use a bidet." It was now my mother's turn to feign deafness while my aunt went into the kitchen and put the kettle on the gas stove. "But we can't actually wash those areas thoroughly," she continued. "Maybe we can wash inside our ears but the inside of our ears isn't lined with, what's the word, mucous membrane."

"What about our noses?" I asked.

"Yes, the nose does produce mucous, but even though our nostrils are lined with mucous membrane, that doesn't really count because we don't wash our noses—we actually pick that part of our bodies."

"That reminds me, when you were little you used to sit and pick your nose absentmindedly while you were reading a book. Mother would scold you and say that the holes in your nose would grow bigger."

"I don't remember that," retorted my aunt.

"You like cleaning your ears, too, don't you, Auntie?"

"I suppose I do."

"I guess in the long run it's like a variation on self-love," I said.

"That's not quite correct," my aunt replied.

"What do you mean?"

"It's not a variation on self-love. It's self-love itself."

Anyhow, that was my aunt's opinion.

3

The day after the freshman welcome ceremony I went to Ueno Station to see my mother off on the Shinkansen.

"Do you think you'll be okay with your aunt?" she asked, sounding rather worried. "Try not to argue with her. She's a little odd, you know," she said surreptitiously, even though there was no reason for her to lower her voice, before adopting a more theatrical tone.

"If you want to meet your Papa, don't give any thought to me. After all, he is your father. In spite of his faults ... He would probably like to meet you, too. And, one last thing—don't forget to behave yourself. Just make sure you don't do anything that looks bad. We'd all be embarrassed. And it would cause problems for your aunt."

"What are you talking about?"

"You know what I mean. Fancy someone calling you in the middle of the night. Any decent person would find that a bit suspicious."

"Hey, the train's leaving. You'll miss it. Hurry up and board."

"That's so typical of your mother," said my aunt later. "But it's the sort of thing mothers say: 'Don't do anything bad because if you do, I'll be embarrassed.'"

"How could it embarrass my mother if I did something bad?"

"She thinks of you as part of her body," my aunt explained. "It seems to me she actually thinks that you're still there inside her womb—and I don't just mean that you are like a part of her body, I mean she thinks that you are, in actual fact, a real part of her own living body—and because this is how all mothers think, they can't accept their children as separate individuals—so if a daughter does something bad, it's the mother who's embarrassed. In fact, you can probably say that the mother's role is to contain the behavior of her children so that, right from the time that they are infants, it's the mother who disciplines the child. You might even call it a kind of social control."

"Even so," I said. "It doesn't alter the fact that she drives me mad."

"Of course not," said my aunt with a sigh, drinking her second cup of milk tea out of a large mug. "Anyway, maybe not straight away, but before too long you'll find a place of your own to live and set up independently, and when that happens your mother will make a huge fuss, I'm sure, but there's not much we can do about that."

Even though I'm not the sort of person who sticks her nose into other people's private lives, it was obvious that my aunt had her own life to lead, and it was equally clear that my aunt's daily life would be unsettled by my mother's plan—which had me staying with Auntie for a year, after which time my brother would finish high school and come up to Tokyo, so that, whether he managed to get into university or had to spend another year studying to upgrade his marks, according to my mother's thinking, "The two of you will be able to take a flat together and then you can look after Jun'ichi and make his meals." Why, you might ask, would I need to care for my brother? My mother would tell you that it's because he's a boy and will be very busy studying.

Of course, it never occurred to my mother how inconvenient it might be for my aunt to have me there for the year, in spite of the fact that I tried to explain some of the problems that might arise.

"What if she's got a lover or something? Don't you think I'll be in the way?"

Even though my mother clearly hadn't given this any thought, her reaction was, "Well, she probably has." She then added, "Do you know anything about him?"

"Of course not. I'm talking hypothetically. But, if she has, don't you think it'll be a bit awkward?"

"Why?"

"What do you mean 'Why?'? What if he stays the night or something?"

"Of course he wouldn't."

"Be realistic, Mother. What are you talking about? She's not a child, you know. Surely you'd expect her to have a lover, or someone like that. It's what usually happens, isn't it?"

"Well, if you're there, she won't let him stay. Surely you don't think your aunt would be so indiscreet, do you?"

"This is not about Auntie being indiscreet. You're unbelievable, Mother. You just don't get it, do you?"

"But surely she wouldn't let a man stay with her."

"I can't believe I'm hearing this. What on earth's wrong with you?"

"She wouldn't do such a dreadful thing."

"Listen to me, will you? What I am trying to say is that having me stay with her will clearly interrupt her own routine in lots of ways."

"Well, maybe, to some extent. She's had a carefree single lifestyle until now. When you go there she mightn't have quite the same freedom ..."

No matter how I tried to explain, my mother seemed incapable of understanding what I was getting at and insisted that, since I was, after all, my aunt's only niece and since my aunt was single and had no other responsibilities, it shouldn't be too much trouble for her to keep an eye on me.

"She left home when she was young and she's had no commitments ever since. She never did one thing around the house. Everything was left to me," declared my mother.

Later, my aunt got her revenge by writing an essay entitled, "Under Surveillance."

Under Surveillance

Although a mother who learns that her daughter is about to live by herself in Tokyo will issue all sorts of cautions, what really infuriates the child is the mother's justification of these admonitions with the claim that, "Your shame is my shame, you know."

Since a daughter has no time to argue the definition of shame, she generally will instead pretend to agree and, thus, there are few daughters prepared to say, "Mother, you have absolutely no idea that the very reason I'm leaving home is because I just cannot stand the way you force this false shame on our family." And if a young woman should decide to wait until she has made her mother understand the fundamental principle that an unmarried daughter must leave home and live alone, then she is unlikely ever to leave home at all.

One of my friends, a woman in her fifties who is married with no children, has summed up the situation very well as follows: "You know, a mother will only treat her daughter as a mature adult when the younger woman has had a child. It's almost as if a mother thinks that by not giving birth, a daughter is refusing to acknowledge her mother's existence." I agree absolutely.

I came to live in Mejiro about seventeen or eighteen years ago and supported myself with the income from my writing. I was shocked to find that there were many people, including my mother, who really didn't understand that such a way of living was possible. For example, I had a group of friends who were young gay men and we all went back and forth to each other's apartments in our free time. We saw movies, plays and Butoh dance performances together, listened to jazz and went to bars in Shinjuku, and, since in those days there weren't any discos, we went to places called "'go-go' clubs," with names like Space Capsule and Mugen, where it was so expensive we could only order one or two drinks each. Of course, before we knew it we had run out of money, but since we naturally still wanted to go out and enjoy ourselves I once decided to get an advance payment for the manuscript of a brief essay I had handed in a couple of days earlier to a publisher with a system where commissioning editors could get permission from the chief editor to authorize the accounts department to advance cash to writers. Leaving my friends to have coffee in a shop opposite the publishing company, I managed to extract forty or fifty thousand yen's worth of manuscript money from my editor, whereupon, thanking her, I went back to my friends in the coffee shop and we headed to the Ginza for a meal, then on by taxi to Space Capsule where we danced for a while, after which we made our way to a bar in Shinjuku for a few drinks.

Sometime later I had a work appointment with the editor who had arranged my advance. "I heard that you took your boyfriends to a bar in Shinjuku and used the money the editor gave you to pay for their drinks," she said. "Is that really true? Mr. So-and-so (she named the chief editor whom I'd never met) was furious. He said he didn't give you the money for that sort of thing. I don't mind, of course. It's your money. You're free to spend it as you like. But you know what middle-aged men are like. They always find something to complain about. Especially if you do something a bit out of the ordinary." Ah-ha, I thought, so that's what Mother was talking about when she warned me against bringing shame on the family.

If you think this discouraged me from requesting cash advances on my manuscripts then you're absolutely wrong; as well as being completely mystified by the miserable attitude of the chief editor who disapproved of how I spent the money he'd released, I was less than impressed with the interfering woman editor who'd decided to play "mother" and to pass on both his comments and her advice. It's laughable to think that, even today, there are probably old-mother editors and objectionable old men like this pair who, I'm sure, still insist on giving young people "advice" and on meddling meaninglessly in what new young writers decide to put in their first novels.

It seems that when a young woman decides to live by herself, whether she likes it or not, people take it on themselves to keep an eye on her, particularly when it comes to matters of money or relations with men.

Wondering what my mother's position would be on all this, I told her the story of the advance. Her first response was that I'd be better off not drinking in the same bars as the staff of the publishing company. "And, anyway," she added, "you're a girl. So don't go making a spectacle of yourself by drinking too much in public."

We women need to be careful since we are often under surveillance when we least expect it. Whenever I think about the time I began to live by myself in Tokyo, I always recall the incident with the editor—but something similar also happened about then when, not long after I visited Kyoto and went for a walk through the Shijo Kawaramachi district with a married male friend whom I had known since kindergarten and who was then living in Kyoto, a woman editor confided to me, rather uncomfortably, that she'd heard some gossip about me. "Someone told me you were walking down the main street of Kyoto with a young man. I said it couldn't be true," she assured me, adding, "There are plenty of people who like to spread rumors, even in the publishing business." Although it was clear that she thought I would deny the story, I just nodded instead and made her even more uncomfortable by replying, "Sure, that was me."

I wonder if young women who live alone in Tokyo these days are still under surveillance in this way. ℘

The night after mother left there was a phone call from "Papa."

When father still lived at home, he was never known as "Papa" because, even though it wasn't fashionable, both my brother and I just called him "Dad." My aunt told me that when she and Mother were children, they originally called my grandparents, "Mommy and Daddy," but that once they were in middle school this became, "Mother and Father," in spite of the fact that our grandparents had simply called their own parents plain old "Mom and Dad." So my aunt had a theory that it was a combination of nostalgia and working class chic that made my parents insist that my brother and I also call them "Mom and Dad."

My mother's substitution of "Papa" for "Dad" came when I was in the fifth grade in primary school about a year after my father had left home. The story my mother told my brother and me was that Father had gone to a hotel in Tokyo to study new trends in the hospitality business. My brother, who was only in Year Two, was still very naïve and, because it was around the time of the oil crisis when there was often news about how the economy was pretty depressed even for seasonal laborers, he learnt the word "seasonal laborer" from the television and caused my mother acute embarrassment by telling everyone that Dad was a seasonal laborer, a mistake that she would predictably insist on correcting. "Of course he's not," she would say tensely. "He's in Tokyo studying." But after about a year she came home from one of her visits to Tokyo with a computer game and a tape recorder for my brother and me, whereupon she clasped the two of us to her breast, one in each arm, in a rather alarming fashion, and after an oppressive silence and a teary embrace of the sort that could not avoid making any child anxious, told us that she and my father would be getting a divorce.

"Your dear Papa wants to live his own life," she said dramatically, although it took us a while to realize that this "Papa" she was talking about was actually our Dad. Even though her announcement was followed by the expected catharsis of my mother and little brother in tears, since Dad had been absent for a year already anyway, we quickly accepted the situation and, before long, slipped into a routine which saw us stay at Dad's place in Tokyo for a few days every summer and winter holiday.

"I thought we might have a meal together to celebrate your going to university," Dad suggested when he rang. "Your mother's gone home, hasn't she? Ask Chieko to come along too. It's not much, but it'll thank her for all her help."

I checked the time and place with my aunt, but as soon as I hung up she said, "Damn. I've just realized that I've got something on then. Can you ring your father back and see if he minds changing the day?" When I rang Dad's apartment, someone answered the phone with a very strange voice that was sort of artificial and shrill, but husky at the same time, so that you couldn't really tell if it was a woman or a man. "Fukao residence," said the voice. Since this was father's name there was no doubt that I had the right number, but, while I knew that Dad lived with some woman, I was still surprised by the voice because I'd never met a woman who talked like that before.

"What a weird voice that woman has. It sounds a bit creepy—just like some old geisha." "Ah," my aunt laughed in reply, "it's Madame Koharu, your father's ... " my aunt pointed her little finger in the air giving the sign for a lover. "I didn't realize that person was still there. You two haven't met, have you?"

"What's she like?" I asked, dying to know. "Don't tell me she worked in *that* sort of business. What was she? A geisha? A blowzy old waitress in some nasty bar?"

"Mmm," said my aunt, avoiding the question, "you must be the daughter of an inn family because most girls your age these days wouldn't have a clue what you're talking about."

Curious to find out more, I did my best to press my aunt for further information. "Well, it seems to me that no regular woman talks like that. But you've met her, haven't you?"

"I have, in fact," she replied. "But you're wrong about the business background. Your father's partner is a flower artist. He'll introduce you if he wants the two of you to meet."

"A flower artist? I wonder if she'll come to dinner?"

"Probably not. A nice person, though. A cat-lover, too."

" A cat-lover?? Mom hates cats."

"Does she?" Auntie asked vaguely. Because my aunt had lived with my mother for twenty years or so it was impossible for her not to know that my mother had a cat allergy and hated cats, but I knew by now that what she really meant by this sort of response was that she didn't want to talk about it any more.

University life was nothing special; all the students, me included, walked around with stupid looks on their faces, and because I had no motivation whatsoever, I would just walk home after classes, map in hand, make some dinner when I arrived, have a meal with my aunt, and watch a bit of TV—my aunt only watched NHK because she hated loud commercials— then take a bath and read one of the spy stories or mystery novels crammed into my aunt's bookshelves and, sometimes, if the book was really exciting, read the whole thing till the end and go to sleep so late that I couldn't wake up next morning and then had to skip university that day, which really didn't matter as there were no decent lectures anyway.

In fact, you could say that, since nothing of actual interest ever happened at university, every day was drably routine and predictable and, because I had no intention of joining any of the inane clubs or societies with their slick advertising posters for new students, I spent my lunch times eating in the dining hall—which had a sign at the entrance written in Latin saying "Suppress your desire"—and talking to the boys and girls in my class, all of whom were pretty boring, except for one student, a very short girl who wore glasses with red plastic frames and was a bit eccentric but very entertaining. Once, when she saw me reading a collection of essays that I'd bought because I liked the close-up photo of a big tabby cat that was on the cover, this girl came up and snatched the book away.

"What's going on here? What are you doing in this photo, Tora-maru?" she cried, looking up at me and then asking, "Can I have the cover of this book?"

"No way," I replied, taken aback.

"Why not??"

"Buy your own copy. I bought it because I liked it."

"Don't be so mean," said the short girl with the glasses. "I'm broke this month. My Mom had to break into her secret savings to pay my tuition fees. Couldn't you just give it to me?"

"No, I couldn't."

"But this cat is the spitting image of my Tora-maru." When the short girl said this, I gave in and, reluctantly removing the cover from the book, handed it over. The other students who were sitting at the table eating their hamburgers and fries, mountains of noodles, and chocolate sundaes, all stared contemptuously at the girl and, later, someone—I can't remember her name—who'd come from a posh private girls' school told me with a frown on her tastefully made up face that the short girl was strange. "And immature," she added.

The next day the short girl thanked me by offering me a free ticket to an advance screening of *Pauline à la plage*, directed by Eric Rohmer, that she'd won from the magazine, *City Road*, but since my aunt had already been given tickets, I told the girl to keep it and go and see the movie herself.

"I'd actually planned to tell you how boring, difficult and uninteresting the movie was to make you say you didn't want the ticket," she said, smiling slyly. "It looks like we're going to be friends," she added.

"If you like," I replied.

Because my aunt had to buy some manuscript paper at Itoya Stationer's in the Ginza, we decided to meet Dad at the Café de France in the underground eatery below Meitetsu Melsa, one of the big department stores in the Ginza. The stationery turned out to be quite heavy so I had to carry the parcel for my aunt who was doing a lot of complaining. "It's handy enough to meet at Melsa if you take the Yurakucho Line from Ikebukuro, but from there to the French restaurant your father booked for us is quite a long way," she grumbled. "Didn't he say it's behind the Shiseido building?" She'd already made a fuss at the stationer's when she discovered that she'd left her shopping coupons at home. "I easily had enough for about 800 yen's credit!" she cried in annoyance at the top of her voice. Embarrassed, I tried to calm her down. "Everyone has their own quirks," she retorted. "I happen to enjoy saving money with shopping vouchers." I let it drop as it was hardly worth an argument and said instead, "I don't believe how heavy this paper is," but my aunt was unsympathetic and merely replied, "And the fact that I have to fill it up with my own writing makes it even heavier." When my father caught up with us at the entrance of Café de France and heard her laments he just nodded sympathetically instead of saying hello and then made an unsuccessful attempt to demonstrate his knowledge of youth fashion by turning to me and saying "Well, look at you. You're just like a São Paulo student." I sighed inwardly.

For an aperitif, my father ordered a glass of Anisette—a liqueur with the same smell as the seeds in rye bread that turns milky when added to water and which my father always drank before a meal because he said it helped his digestive system— my aunt ordered a beer and, although it momentarily occurred to me to emulate the defiance of the young Beauvoir, who apparently ordered restaurant food in reverse order, that is, with dessert first and aperitif last, I decided that this would be a bit affected so had a dry sherry instead. Of course, I had never drunk dry sherry and I only ordered it because this is what people in English novels always drink, but I discovered that it actually tasted quite good. When my father announced that the current drink in vogue for young women was some mixture of gooseberry juice and white wine, my aunt and I pretended not to hear and I made a point of forgetting what it was called as soon as he said it.

Dad soon noticed that my navy blue jogging shoes didn't really go with the classic grey flannel Ralph Lauren suit that my mother had bought to celebrate my starting university and he became quite excited by the idea that he should buy me a new pair of shoes to commemorate my university entrance.

"Do you think I need new shoes?" I asked ironically. "I suppose these aren't really suitable for eating out—although I think I look quite stylish, sort of like a New York career woman." When I said this, my aunt frowned and commented, "Don't go copying a career woman if you want to look stylish because the worst thing a woman can do is to try to look like a man." I was rather bemused by this comment and wondered how she could accuse others of being conservative when she was able to come out with something like that herself.

Anyway, the three of us ended up going to the upmarket shopping complex, THE GINZA, in order to buy some shoes. Dad looked a bit uncomfortable when my aunt and I both said that we had never been anywhere before that sold such expensive things, and he claimed defensively that he'd only bought the odd small thing there.

"Like an Armani sweater or a pair of cufflinks?" asked my aunt.

"No, no," said Dad. "Just paper-clips and that sort of thing."

Of course, I couldn't help being a bit excited by the fascinating array of fabulous goods, all very expensive-looking and each glowing softly under the caress of the showcase lighting; but, on the other hand, I just was not in the mood to play the part of the daughter being taken by her father to shop for luxury goods. Dad, however, was completely swept up in his role because you have to remember that, like all hotel managers, he has a theatrical bent, and he was determined to play the part of a rich and stylish middle-aged father by having an endless assortment of shoes brought out, one pair after the other, and making me try them on and walk around the shop. Since I normally bought my shoes on sale and was happy as long as the size, design and price were okay, this made me feel very uncomfortable. And Dad, who was really getting on my nerves, was stupid enough to be playing the part of the father in *Bonjour Tristesse*. To sum it up, he was being as self-opinionated as the father in *The Goddess*, a popular novel by Mishima Yukio that I had read as a child—I was always reading the books my aunt left packed in boxes in the store room—who was overjoyed that he'd trained the daughter he adored to choose a cocktail to match the color of her outfit. Later that night, when we were back home in Mejiro, my aunt and I had a good laugh at all three—my father, the father in the novel, and the man who could write such melodramatic nonsense.

But at THE GINZA my father ended up buying me a pair of very stylish, black cordovan leather shoes with laces (that cost 38,000 yen!)—although personally I would rather have had the pink and grey Tokio Kumagai pumps that looked like elephants with ears and a trunk on the top of the shoe that flapped about as you walked but which father refused to buy because he claimed I needed something more practical. "You'd soon get sick of fun shoes like that," he said. And since he also vetoed my second choice, a pair of scarlet shoes identical to the ones that Audrey Hepburn wore in the movie, *Sabrina*, I had to be happy with a pair of conservative lace-ups.

Because my father wanted to show off, he offered to buy a pair of shoes for my aunt. "Okay, thanks," she said. "I'll have these." I bit my lip, mortified to see her choose the scarlet Sabrina shoes, but, as Father was settling the bill, she took me aside and said quietly with a smile, "Our feet are the same size, so I'll give them to you later." When, overcome at her generosity and feeling a little guilty, I offered to swap the Sabrinas for the cordovan lace-ups, my aunt's face lit up momentarily. "Maybe I will," she said tentatively, but then reconsidered. "No," she said firmly. "You take those as well." Although I felt a bit bad, I had to confess that I quite liked the feeling of opulence this shoe ownership gave me, realizing that not only had I inherited my parents' socially pretentious genes but that I was also just plain greedy.

"I feel a bit stuck-up, wearing these shoes that are easily five or six times the value of what I've worn for the last nineteen years," I said cheerfully. "And to top it off," I added to my aunt with a shopping bag from THE GINZA in each hand, "I've ended up with two pairs of shoes." One bag held my old shoes while the other had the shoes my aunt said she would give me.

"When I was your age," my aunt said, "shoes from Boutique Osaki were all the rage and a friend of mine who had a part-time job at your father's hotel took everything he'd saved from his job and spent it all on a pair of shoes for his girlfriend."

"Yes, I remember too," my father joined in. "He was a very handsome boy who looked wonderful in the hotel's livery uniform. He was just like one of those lovely young men you see in Vietnamese restaurants in Paris."

My father then began telling us how the boy asked him to choose shoes from Boutique Osaki in Harajuku. Even though my father said that shoes should be tried on before being bought, this was out of the question since this pretty Vietnamese-looking young man had set his heart on his girlfriend untying the ribbon around a gift box, taking off the lid, and folding back the tissue paper to discover a pair of black suede pumps. "Mr. Fukao," the boy said to my father, "you have such excellent taste; I would really appreciate your advice." It seemed to me that boys who ask for help from older men when choosing clothes or accessories for their lovers are usually closet gays, but when I said this to my father he just smiled and continued, "Well, anyway, once we arrived at the shop, I didn't feel like choosing anything at all. Do you want to know why?"

As we walked down the Ginza street, my father kept talking against the noise of the traffic while doing his best to avoid bumping into people coming from the other direction, but because my hearing is not so good in the left ear I don't like having to talk while I'm walking. It's not too bad with someone of your own height, but Dad's taller than I am, so even with my good right ear it was quite tiring having to listen to words tumbling down from above while filtering out the hustle and bustle of the street.

"What did you say?" I asked. I had, in fact, actually heard what he said and only asked because I was so irritated. "I said, why do think I suddenly lost interest in helping the young man choose a pair of shoes?" my father replied in a loud voice as we arrived at the building in which the French restaurant he'd booked was located. "Here we are. It's here," he said, looking back over his shoulder to my aunt. An affected middle-aged couple, wearing expensive-looking clothes, stood aloofly waiting for the elevator and as soon as my father saw them he rushed up and claimed them, and then introduced my aunt and me—although I'm not sure why because they certainly weren't interested in talking to us. The couple we met were both haute couture fashion designers whose names even I had seen in magazines like *Vogue*, but since neither my aunt nor I had the slightest bit of interest in that sort of thing, it was the first time that we had ever met people in that line of work, and they clearly likewise had no idea about minor novelists like my aunt—although, mind you, this certainly didn't excuse the manner in which the woman gave a disgraceful display of running her eye over us from head to toe and contemptuously scrutinizing my aunt and me as if she was conducting an inspection and grading us. When I complained later, my aunt said that fashion designers are very practiced at ruthlessly judging people by the clothes they wear. "I've been looked at like that plenty of times," she said. "I'm quite happy if they reject me as a future client. It means I don't have to have anything to do with them," she explained laughing. "And anyway," she continued, "when I read other people's writing, I judge them equally ruthlessly whether or not they're amateurs, but, while there might be an ugly side to being a professional, there's no doubt she could have been a bit more sophisticated in the way that she dismissed us—Parisians are much more skilled at that sort of thing, you know, and I'm sure that someone from Paris would have been more subtle." Meanwhile Dad had apparently forgotten about abandoning the boy who had asked for his advice on shoes and started telling us about the French restaurant that we were about to go to.

"The owner of this restaurant," Dad explained, "was once the chef in the Japanese restaurant in my hotel. His nephew studied cooking in Lyon. So you'll be eating something different here. You can call it nouvelle cuisine, or new Japanese-style cooking. Either way, it's a delightful combination of the uncle's Japanese cooking and the nephew's French influence. And all presented in a very relaxed, informal setting. There is an excellent wine and sake list and, at this time of the year, they serve fresh sea-bream and shellfish which can be ordered as either sashimi or in a salad entrée with an olive oil dressing. Their olive oil is specially ordered by the barrel from a farming family estate near Manton, in the south of France."

He went on and on the way he always did with his usual never-ending monologue; and although a kind person might say that, because of his occupation, he's developed a sophisticated and refined understanding of food and drink, I would say that he's made it his business to peddle bad taste leisure to the nouveau riche—my mother, on the other hand, does her best to sell home-style comfort and local color—but the point is that whenever I dine out with my father, I find myself being subjected to one of his interminable commentaries. To put it bluntly, he's a pretentious old fool who insists on teaching me things that I don't need to know.

The table in the restaurant was covered with a pink linen tablecloth and serviettes arranged in misshapen ("interesting" would be too much of a compliment) serviette rings—the "art work" of the owner whose hobby was pottery—all set up in an interior that was a unique combination of Japanese and Southern French styles that curiously felt quite familiar because it was almost identical to a Mediterranean restaurant, called La Bohème, run back home by an old classmate of my aunt's, the daughter of a seafood-manufacturing businessman, who'd gone to Italy to study voice and to become a beautiful opera singer but who had been a total failure and had been forced to return to Japan. During her annual summer vacation trips to Italy she'd gone to flea markets and folk-craft markets where she'd bought all sorts of old junk that now totally cluttered up her restaurant and, though I'm no connoisseur, I can tell you that nothing matched and there was nothing of any value.

"Look at this," I said to my aunt. "It's just like La Bohème."

"Yes, it is, isn't it?" she said, laughing. "You know, Miss Kurihara" (this was the name of her classmate who'd had to abandon plans of an opera career) "thought she looked just like Claudia Cardinale," adding for my benefit, "that is the name of an Italian actress, you know," although this was unnecessary since I had, in fact, seen movies on television with Cardinale.

My aunt then launched into the sort of gossip in which she and my mother indulged whenever there was mention of the unfortunate Miss Kurihara, for, in spite of their many differences of opinion, on this point both my aunt and my mother were incorrigible.

"At first she thought she looked like Cardinale," one would begin, "but after she saw Antonioni's *Red Desert* she desperately wanted to be like Monica Vitti so she changed her image from primitive seduction to ennui and existential angst because Monica Vitti's selling point, you know, was letting her mouth hang open slightly in abandon."

"That's right," the other would reply, eager for Miss Kurihara's blood. "I read somewhere that, in order to capture that look, Antonioni would have her count backwards before the camera began to roll."

"Yes, I've heard that too. But in Kurihara's case, there was no need to count—because she was always a bit dim-witted. She looked like that naturally. "

"True. Although for someone so stupid she doesn't do too badly in business."

"She is certainly not bad with money, although she's got plenty of problems with men."

The only time my aunt and my mother seemed to get on was when they were running someone down. What I found really strange, however, was the fact that my mother went to the movies when she was young because this was something I would certainly never have guessed from her present image as a sensible businesswoman.

Although Father knew nothing about either Miss Kurihara or La Bohème, he joined in the conversation undeterred. "Yes, Antonioni," he said. "I remember. Italian neo-realism." Since my aunt contemptuously declined to reply to this misinformed comment, I took it upon myself to let him know he was wrong—although I had never seen an Antonioni movie—but he just ignored me, which was typical of both my parents who would suddenly become hard of hearing whenever confronted with something not to their liking.

"Oh, by the way," he said, changing the subject, "to go back to the story I was telling before, the girlfriend's shoe size was 25.5. I was so appalled that I lost interest in helping the boy choose something for her. I can't bear women with oversized feet," he continued. "They are such great big unattractive creatures."

"I suppose so," I answered.

Because no one was listening to his story, Father was looking a bit chagrined, but, hospitality trade veteran that he is, he soon recovered and called out to the restaurant owner in a knowing, familiar voice, "What have you got for us today?" My mother does exactly the same thing whenever she eats out but I am always embarrassed by the faux intimacy that is part of both the hospitality and entertainment trades.

Dinner finished without too much conversation, which was partly the result of my tiring of listening to the nonstop affected exchange that took place between my father and the restaurateur as they chose the menu, although, to tell the truth, since my father and I rarely engaged in animated or natural conversation, by the time we were drinking our espresso I was exhausted from the strain.

"When you leave university, do you think you'll take over your mother's business?" Father asked as he drank his liqueur.

"Absolutely not," I replied.

"So even though it's operated for a hundred years or so, the business will come to an end with your mother?"

"I don't see any problem with that," I said.

"What do you want to do, then?" asked Father.

"Well, I'm not sure. But looking at Auntie, it seems that being a novelist is not too stressful. Maybe that would be okay."

"You're right," said my aunt. "It's not too stressful, but there's not much future in it."

"I don't know," said my father. "Not everyone can write a novel. I think you're being a bit superficial." He turned to my aunt for support. "Creative work is not all that easy, is it?" he asked.

"It's quite easy, actually," she said, making it my father's turn now to be nonplussed.

5

Later that evening, after we'd returned home and I was in bed reading a book, the phone rang. The caller, who seemed to be drunk, began to go on and on. "You've been avoiding me, haven't you? Why won't you meet me?" he sniveled. Intensely irritated, I stopped him short. "Listen here," I said, "I have never once said I was in love with you and I can't bear people who blubber like this." My aunt was in the living room drinking whiskey and reading a Yamada Fūtarō novel. She raised her eyebrows and grinned. "You young women seem to think you have a right to be cruel. Mind you, you obviously have to speak plainly to get the message across to these sorts of self-opinionated young men. They take a while to catch on, don't they?" I smiled back at her and took a small sip of whiskey. "If he rings again, would you mind saying I'm not here?" I asked.

"I'm not sure if I can. I can only lie when I don't really mean to," she answered.

"You mean you don't know when you're telling a lie?"

"Maybe I do lie deliberately now and again."

"Well, no matter, I'd really like you to tell him I'm not here. He's such a pain."

"I don't want you to think I'm unnecessarily standing on principle here," said my aunt, "but, you know, telling a lie is not really all that helpful."

Although I had to agree with her, I still said, "That might be true. But, no matter how stupid he is, if you tell him I'm not here five or six times in a row he'll eventually get the message, won't he?" I couldn't bear the thought of him ringing again and boring me silly with his dreary talk.

"It's been rather a long time since I was in this situation

myself so I really can't say," my aunt replied.

Up until that point I hadn't actually thought too much about whether or not I liked this boy. But now I decided that I definitely disliked him. When he'd first called my aunt's place last summer telling me that he'd asked one of my friends for the number, I'd only gone out with him because I was bored with studying for exams and was a bit curious to find out what he was like. Even though I'd clearly made the wrong decision, there was nothing that could be done about it.

The young man I was doing my best to avoid was the only son of a family that ran a small seafood business. Not that you would have known this to hear him talk because he managed to make everything he did sound immensely grand and important. Sometimes, as a way of trying to make me believe he was smart enough to enjoy doing difficult things, he'd start to tell me about the economic theory course he was studying at college—as if I cared. He also liked to make a big fuss about some country town in England where his university had sent him for a short-term exchange program—in fact, the way he never stopped talking about how wonderful *his* university was made him sound more like a man in his forties talking about the company he worked for than an ordinary student—in fact, he had a whole repertoire of petty middle-aged topics of conversation, which included proudly telling me that the girls at *his* university were "highly conscious of fashion labels." Once, when he was sounding off like this in a coffee shop, I suddenly remembered that in the past we'd nicknamed him Crab Stick—partly because of his father's business but also because he was such a jumped-up pretentious little moron. After he finished on the girls at his college, he started waffling on again about his month-long exchange program in the dormitory of the English university he'd been to that no one had ever heard of—just like the one in David Lodge's *Changing Places*—although he managed to make it sound like some incredible privilege to be there. In other words, he's a lot like his aunt, Miss Kurihara, the failed opera singer from the fake Italian restaurant; but while she's stupid enough to worship anything Italian, he likes to put England on a pedestal.

The last time I saw Crab Stick he offered to buy me dinner so we met at a coffee shop at Mejiro—though I have no idea why, given that we were eating at Roppongi, which is nowhere near Mejiro. Anyway, it was a really hot day and to get there we had to take a train, change to the subway right at the peak of the rush hour and, after leaving Roppongi station, walk for ages down the main road with the afternoon sun beating straight into our faces. Crab Stick chose some Italian restaurant famous for ravioli with a wild rabbit sauce, but since we'd worked so hard to come all the way to Roppongi, I made him take me after the meal to Cine Vivant to see Jean-Luc Godard's *Prénom Carmen,* during which he promptly fell asleep. While he was sleeping I realized he had a rather strong body odor. "I thought this movie was about Carmen," he said when he woke up as the movie was ending. "How come there were no flamenco dancing or bullfights?" It was just the sort of comment I would have expected him to come out with. After that, Crab Stick took me to some famous disco and, eventually, to a bar with an ultramodern Art Nouveau sort of interior which he claimed had been featured in a couple of magazine articles and where, insisting that we drink Scotch and water "without ice," he ordered a weird fermented soybean omelet dish garnished with spicy white radish shoots and baby spring onions. Finally, he took me all the way home in a taxi quite a distance back to Mejiro, having paid for everything for the two of us. "You're pretty well-off, aren't you?" I asked enviously since I could only dream of being as cashed up as he was. "My parents spoil me a bit because I'm the only son and I'll take over the family business," he said, trying to play down his wealth. "It doesn't really mean that I'm all that rich." I was just about to say that he didn't have to tell me what I already knew when he took my hand and said in a sort of husky voice, "I've liked you for a long time." I didn't want to seem juvenile by pulling away, so I sat there with him holding my hand which, because he was sweating so heavily, became quite damp from his moist and clammy palm, so I eventually let go and wiped the moisture off on the sleeve of the pale blue jacket he said he'd bought at Harrods when he was in London. Maybe he mistook this for an expression of my affection because when we arrived at my apartment he got out of the cab and kissed me. He was a little drunk and I was quite drunk, and, even though his body odor was a bit strong, he had nice soft lips and his breath wasn't too bad, so the kiss on the whole could have been a lot worse.

That's what had happened when we last went out together but I'd soon forgotten all about it. At the time I did feel a bit of feminist disquiet at having so much money spent on me and even thought of offering to pay my share; but it was an expensive outing and, given that my miserly little monthly allowance would have been gone in one hit, I decided to accept the benefits of a paid meal as my due, something I'm sure you'll agree with once you understand why.

My mother's inn was an important customer of Kurihara Fisheries, the business operated by Crab Stick's father, so, as I told Crab Stick when he rang a few days later, I decided that the cost of our outing should be acquitted against the company's entertainment budget. "Ask your father for a refund," I said. "I'd feel much better if he reimbursed you."

The next day I woke up with a hangover and, because I didn't feel like going to school with an aching head, I had a raw egg—I remembered my aunt saying that this was a good hangover cure—and then soaked in a nice warm bath for about half an hour. I felt pretty down in the dumps and all sorts of miserable thoughts swirled around in my head.

I put some Bub bath salts in the water and lay there gazing absentmindedly at the tiny bath salt bubbles that collected around my pubic hair and the hair on my arms and legs. Although the sight of my body hair covered in lines of myriad little bubbles, like sea grass after a codfish deposits her roe, made me feel even more depressed, I remembered that at least one good thing had happened the day before—namely that Father had bought me two pairs of shoes from THE GINZA— and this made me feel a little bit brighter and even gave me enough energy to wash my hair. The *sauvage* style I'd been wearing was starting to bore me and I was thinking about whether or not to get my hair cut very short, which would also have made it easier to wash. After I had a bath and dried my hair I realized I was pretty hungry, but I decided that before eating I just had to take my new shoes out of the box and try them on in front of the mirror. They were the fabulous kinds of shoes that everyone would admire and the red Sabrina shoes, which suited me perfectly, looked simply wonderful on my slender, gleaming, freshly bathed legs. Even though neither my aunt nor I ever wore shoes in the house I went into the kitchen still in the Sabrinas feeling very satisfied. Lots of people these days scorn the word "kitchen," preferring instead to use trendy euphemisms like "food preparation area," but I think those newfangled expressions are such a joke, so I went into the plain old kitchen where I was just starting to eat the ham and cucumber sandwich I'd made myself and have my cup of tea, when my aunt, who'd been asleep, got out of bed and joined me.

She stood there drowsily with her hair standing on end like a hedgehog, rubbing the sleep from the corner of her eyes. "Make me a cup, too, will you?" she said with a yawn as she put one hand into the hem of her pajama top to scratch her tummy. As I watched her, I thought, "What great lives novelists have." It was all such a change from my mother who, probably because of her work, had never been seen at the breakfast table without make-up or a properly fitted kimono. My aunt, on the other hand, always wore pajamas or cotton trainers unless she was going out, changing back into pajamas the minute she came home where she would loll about, declare how tired she was and then have a read of one of the magazines that are always piled up around her apartment. Around half past six or so, she'd say, "I think I'm getting hungry." So she'd start to make dinner and then watch the seven o'clock NHK news and weather report; and, even though it's exactly the same, she'd also watch the weather report on the nine o'clock news, inevitably making some complaint about the forecast.

The short girl with spectacles from my class was always reading books and was a fan of my aunt's novels. Now, although all my classmates thought this girl was really eccentric, even she would have been pretty shocked by the casual nature of my aunt's everyday routine. The image the short girl had of my aunt was a pretty laughable one of a self-disciplined sort of person who was above all the hustle and bustle of the world.

"I suppose," the short girl mused, "that, even though the two of you are related, she's quite different from you."

Then she asked courteously in a way that was very out of character for her, "By the way, I wonder if it would be okay if I came around for a visit?"

"Sure," I replied. "I don't mind. Anytime is fine."

She looked doubtful. "What about your aunt?" she asked. "Won't she be annoyed if the boarder starts bringing her friends home?"

Although my hangover had cleared, the thought of Crab Stick made me feel quite unwell—it really gave me the creeps to think he was so keen on me. After his call the night before, my aunt had teased, "Ah, what an innocent youth he is. There's not many like him these days." I was only too aware of his motives and, I can tell you now, there was nothing innocent about them.

"So he's the boy from the Kurihara Fisheries family, is he?" reflected my aunt. "I see. I've met the father and the younger sister. Kurihara Senior is a notorious womanizer, you know. His wife was always complaining about his carryings-on to your grandmother."

"I know," I replied. "He set up his mistress or his girlfriend, or whatever she was, to run the little fish shop near the station. You know the place. It's a Kurihara outlet shop. He got her pregnant and she had a daughter who was in my high school class."

"Well," said my aunt, "it might sound like a cliché, but when the father runs around like that it's not unusual for the son to be doubly straight and sincere."

"Yes, that's exactly what he's like—it's unbearable," I said. "I've been too embarrassed to tell you this, but he actually told me he'd asked me out because he was thinking of marrying me. Can you believe it?"

"Wha-at!!" cried my aunt, looking shocked. "Me related to Kurihara Fisheries? That'll be the day." She laughed uproariously and continued. "You know, your mother has always loathed that boy's father. Even when he was only in his thirties or so, she would call him a dirty old man. And he was. There was only ever one thing on his mind. He spent his time like some teenager endlessly telling tired old dirty jokes that everyone had heard a thousand times. But why on earth is his son so keen to marry you?"

"Well, good question," I said to my aunt. "Crab Stick says it's because he loves me. He told me he'd always admired me from afar," I explained. "But who marries just for love? Do you think my parents would have married just because they loved each other? I don't think so. They married for the sake of the business, even though things fell apart in the end." Then I added as an aside, "Not that I know anything about Dad and his present wife, though."

"His wife? I suppose we can use the word 'wife,'" my aunt said vaguely. "So what did Crab Stick say then?" she asked, urging me to continue. I'd noticed that whenever the subject of the woman who lived with my father arose, a look of both ambiguity and embarrassment seemed to flash across my aunt's face. "It's okay, you know," I said to her, trying to let her know I didn't mind if she talked about my father's situation. "I don't have any grudge against Dad. Men run out on their families all the time." I then went back to telling her about the disturbingly calculating way that Crab Stick had managed to dream up a romantic plan that would also benefit his business future.

It had all started when he came to see me at my grandmother's house during the winter vacation and asked if I had time to go with him for a bit of a drive. Now, I had just had a huge run-in with my mother and was feeling pretty annoyed, so I said, "Sure. Why not?" And why, you'll probably ask, did Mother and I argue? Basically, because that woman is just impossible.

It was close to exam time and I'd slept in after studying all night. When I woke up I went into the kitchen to make myself something to eat. I'd fried a frozen hamburger patty and was making myself a nice hamburger sandwich when my brother came in. "Hey, make me one too, will you?" he said. "If you want something to eat, make it yourself," I said annoyed. Just then, my mother happened to come home for a moment from the inn next door where she'd been working. "You can't expect Jun'ichi to be frying his own hamburger," she said. "You're in the middle of doing yours right now, aren't you? It will only take a minute to make a second one." Now, if that had been all she'd said, there wouldn't have been a problem. But, just as I was about to start eating the sandwich, complete with shredded cabbage and pickles, and take a sip of the tea I'd also made for myself, she added, "Yours'll get cold while you make Jun'ichi's. Give this one to your brother and make another for yourself." She pushed the tray with the sandwich over to her son. "Hey, wait a minute," I said raising my voice. "That's mine." My brother seemed a bit taken aback by my tone. "Okay, okay," he said. "You eat first."

"You bet I'll eat first," I snarled.

As I stuck my head in the newspaper and took a bite of the sandwich, my mother gave one of her ostentatious sighs.

"Is making your brother something to eat so much to ask?" she said, exhaling the smoke from her cigarette. "What's wrong with letting him eat first?"

"If it's so easy," I said, "then why can't he make it himself?"

"Girls," my mother declared, "have an obligation to look after their little brothers. What are you thinking, asking him to do it himself?"

"You *are* joking, aren't you?" I said. "Maybe you haven't noticed but he's not a baby. He has no difficulty masturbating so I'm sure he can fry a hamburger by himself! I don't see any need to run after him."

"Don't you dare use language like that," my mother cried, becoming even more infuriated and launching into one of her interminable sexist sermons—at which point Crab Stick arrived, escorted into the dining room by Grandmother. "There's someone here to see you," Grandmother said to me, whereupon my mother, overcome with the desire to impress, grabbed my arm and shoved me up the stairs. "You look terrible," she hissed at me. "Hurry up and get changed." She then turned to Crab Stick, positioning herself in front of the stairs in order to conceal the vision of her daughter's pajama-clad form from the eyes of the visitor. "I'm so sorry," she said sweetly, "she was up studying until late last night. She's just got up, dreadful girl that she is," she added obsequiously, doing her best to keep up appearances.

Now, it wasn't as if I had just stepped out of the bath and was wearing nothing but a bath-towel or a pair of panties; in fact, pajamas seemed to me to be quite a respectable item of clothing. I might have only lived in a little local town, but we girls in the know read fashion magazines like *Olive* and even wore cute pajama tops as ordinary clothes when we went out. The cotton flannel pajamas I had on at the time were sort of like leisure wear. "You remember them," I said to my aunt. "My Felix the Cat print pajamas with the long top. You nearly died when you heard the price." "I still can't believe that anyone would pay as much as 12,000 yen for a pair of pajamas," said my aunt. "Anyway, what happened then?"

As I told my aunt, nothing really happened after that, except that I was so annoyed with my mother that I went for a drive with Crab Stick. When the bullet train came to Niigata, new restaurants sprang up everywhere on the esplanade along the coast. There were all those white American colonial–style buildings, you know the sort that everyone goes to. Anyway, we went to one of those, the kind of place that had real lace curtains instead of synthetic ones. It was a seafood restaurant called something like Porto Bello, a bit like a European-style pension that the slightly old-fashioned sort of girl who buys *Non-no* would just love. And even though it was all very Mediterranean, the menu was that American West Coast–style for people who like health food. In actual fact, it was a branch of Miss Kurihara's La Bohème. Anyway, that's where he took me. And it was there that the precious Mr. Crab Stick boasted about his vision for developing the restaurant that we went to and also told me about his vision for our joint future.

"His car? I've got no idea," I said to my aunt. "I'm not interested in cars so I can't tell you what sort it was. But he stroked it so proudly I'm sure it must have been expensive."

"The new trend," said Crab Stick, "is for this sort of bright, well-lit décor and atmosphere as well as an understanding of the importance of health food. These days, there's not such a gap between what people want in Tokyo and your medium-sized provincial city. Sure, this place would be okay like this for quite a while, but if you run a business with the same old concept you'll be left behind," he explained knowingly, sipping the Calpis and Perrier he'd ordered—which actually didn't taste too bad, although, of course, it was just the same as a Calpis soda.

"By the way," he said. "Will you take over the family business? I wonder if there's been any talk of adopting a husband into the family."

My reply was pretty predictable. "It hasn't entered my head," I said. What I meant, of course, was that I would rather die than consider such an idea, but Crab Stick, who wasn't actually taking notice of anything I said, just kept detailing more and more of his plan. The marriage proposal that he put to me was a truly pragmatic, overtly scheming even, mix of business and family life convenience. He spoke with the confidence of someone determined to do well at a job interview for a big company— I'm sure you've seen the sort of thing on those documentaries they show on NHK where the camera first zooms in for a close-up of the spotty face of some anxious young man, then cuts to hands folded in laps. And, of course, there's always a shot of feet shuffling nervously, which inevitably features some poor creature who's wearing white cotton socks with his dark blue suit. It's always the same. TV cameramen have absolutely no imagination. Anyway, Crab Stick said, "Our marriage would herald a new business era. With a direct connection between Kurihara Fisheries, your inn and these restaurants, we could start a completely new concept that combined food production and distribution with the service industry. I'll make a booking for us to stay together at the Shirahama Hotel in Ise. They run their own farm and have freshly picked vegetables prepared by top class chefs served to your table with fresh seafood." Can I point out here that this man takes himself so seriously that he even uses expressions like "served to your table" in casual conversation? But I digress. "With the bullet train running out here now," he said triumphantly, "there'll soon be a renaissance all along the Sea of Japan coast. Only those with the sensitivity and imagination of youth will succeed in business. And, of course, we'll need to make sure we include a woman's point of view. That'll be crucial."

"Has anyone ever told you that you remind them of a junior version of *President*?" I asked Crab Stick, giving a loud burp that smelt of the hamburger I'd just eaten—I always give a burp that smells like old meat whenever I eat something like ready-made hamburgers or McDonalds. "I'm not the least bit interested in anything that's in that magazine—and, more importantly, I've got even less interest in marrying you because, just now, all I have time to think about is my entrance exams."

"Alright, fair enough," said Crab Stick. "But just keep my idea in mind. You don't have to agree right away. But sooner or later you'll have to start thinking seriously about your future. All I ask is that, when you do, you remember what I've said and give it some thought."

"He's painful, isn't he?" said my aunt who had listened to my story with a grin on her face. Then she said "Well, I think I might have a bath too."

"Would you like something to eat when you finish?" I asked.

"I might just have a beer," she replied. "I'm a bit dehydrated from my hangover." She looked a little uncomfortable and seemed to be making an excuse.

"Miso soup is supposed to be good for a hangover," I suggested.

"But it's easier just to have a beer, isn't it?" she replied. "You just take it out of the fridge and open it."

Of course I had to agree with her.

While my aunt was in the bath, the doorbell rang and I went to answer it thinking it would be a courier delivery from an editor or something but, when I opened the door, there to my surprise stood the short girl in my class whose name was Miss Yoshida.

"What are you doing here?" I asked.

"You told me to come anytime, so here I am," she explained. "But if you're busy, I'll leave."

"We're not busy but my aunt's got a bit of a hangover and she's in the bath at the moment."

"So now's probably not a good time," said Miss Yoshida.

"It's okay," I assured her. "I don't think she's busy today, or should I say today as usual—but don't worry, come on in. What's that? A present?"

"Yeah, but it's nothing special," Miss Yoshida said entering the apartment. "I've brought some flowers. Do you like them? It's a bunch of forget-me-nots and daisies that I asked the florist to make up specially." She looked around curiously, holding the little bouquet tied with a pastel blue ribbon as if it was something precious. "So," she said, "this is what your aunt's place is like."

"It's not the sacred site you might think," I said matter-of-factly.

"Listen, I'm no romantic and I certainly wouldn't think of it as sacred, but it is fascinating to think that this is where she creates all her texts," she said in something of a hushed voice.

I knew that she was an excitable girl who was easily moved but the way that her cheeks became flushed and her eyes shone through the glasses with the gaudy plastic frames bordered on the pathetic.

"I could make you a tea or a coffee," I suggested. "Which would you like?"

"Just water," she said boyishly.

"It's a bit inhospitable just to give you water," I said, laughing at her restraint. "What about a beer instead?" I was aware of sounding just like my mother who was very practiced at receiving guests.

"I couldn't possibly," said Miss Yoshida, her eyes growing

round in shock at my suggestion. "I can't have a beer without even introducing myself to your aunt—it would be different if she had offered me one herself."

"A-ha," I pounced. "So you really do want a beer."

"Well," said Miss Yoshida, "I rode my push-bike here so I can't deny that I'm pretty thirsty."

"My aunt said she'll have a beer when she comes out of the bath, so why don't you wait?"

"Do you think she'll be out soon?" inquired Miss Yoshida. "If she will be, I'll wait."

I went into the bathroom and let my aunt know that the girl in my class I'd told her about had arrived and that she was so excited and thirsty that she wanted to have a beer.

"Oh no!" A cry was heard from the sitting room. "Don't say that! I said I only wanted water," Miss Yoshida said with a groan.

"Tell her to have a drink without me," answered my aunt in a sleepy voice.

"I can't possibly do that," Miss Yoshida insisted.

I was a little nonplussed by her resistance because just the other day when we were hungry after class we went to a noodle shop on our way home to order soba topped with bits of deep-fried batter and on that occasion Miss Yoshida had ordered a beer in a very down-to-earth manner.

"Do you always drink beer at a noodle shop?" I had asked rather inanely, pretty impressed at the ease with which she had placed her order.

"I'd be broke if I did it all the time," she answered. I hadn't really explained what I meant very well but the point I'd been trying to make was that it was usually middle-aged men who ordered beer with their soba and that it looked a bit out of place to see a slightly built girl who wore glasses do this.

"Actually, this is the first time I've ordered beer in a soba shop," she'd explained, seeming then to understand what I meant.

"Really?" I replied.

Now, I don't know whether beer and soba topped with deep-fried batter is an accepted culinary combination but, that day, the heat of the soba and the oily texture of the batter had blended very nicely with the chill of the beer so, with this in mind, I suggested to Miss Yoshida that I order some of this soba to be delivered to my aunt's. However, she didn't reply.

Miss Yoshida had supper with us and stayed until late that evening so, as a result, I ended up overworking my digestive system by drinking alcohol on two consecutive days and, even though I had a new pair of shoes to show off, I lost the opportunity because I skipped university both days. Although that didn't really matter, I did wonder whether or not it was good for me to have too much to drink two days in a row.

6

Miss Yoshida's unexpected visit meant that I missed the chance to tell my aunt anything else about Crab Stick's proposal, but this was no great drama because it wasn't actually all that important. I have to admit that, as a young woman, I am narcissistic enough to consider being young as a privilege to which I have every right. My aunt, who enjoys giving an image of herself as someone getting on in years, would point out that to do so is to mistake one's youth as a kind of natural gift—which is something that I am at least vaguely aware of, though it's also true that in reality it's not possible for anyone to be aware of these things too clearly. Even so, I wouldn't like people to think that being proposed to made me happy, especially when it was only by that stupid young man—I totally refute that claim as unimaginative and a good example of petty bourgeois self-satisfaction.

In the end, Miss Yoshida, who was sweating and red in the face after riding her bike all the way from Nishi-Ochiai, decided to put up with her thirst and wait for my aunt to come out of the bath before having anything to drink.

"You must really enjoy drinking to hold out for a beer rather than have a glass of water," I said.

"Think of me as a small-time hedonist," she said, making her tongue hang out and panting like a dog.

"Do dogs drink beer?" I asked.

"You bet they do," she said.

"Do they eat *kushikatsu* kebabs and *edamame*?"

"Bow-wow," she replied energetically, as I realized that she was even more childish than I'd thought.

My aunt came out of the bath and saw Miss Yoshida barking away cheerily.

"Now that you've made her so happy you'll definitely have to give her some chicken and edamame. There's edamame in the freezer and you can deep fry some kushikatsu kebabs."

"Please don't go to any trouble," said Miss Yoshida, playing the young lady. "I was just having a joke with Momoko—we were pretending to be beer-drinking dogs." It was clear that my aunt took to Miss Yoshida as soon as she heard this comment which, in fact, surprised me a bit.

"Come on," I complained. "Don't make me cook kushikatsu— it's too much trouble and, besides, kushikatsu might be okay with draught beer but they don't go so well with bottled or canned beer," I argued.

"Momoko is right," said Miss Yoshida with a show of super serious politeness and sincerity that made her sound like a cultured young woman from the suburbs. "You really don't need to go to any trouble."

I wondered to myself whom she thought she was trying to impress but must confess that I myself was quite impressed at her hidden talent for polite behavior. In the end I agreed to boil the edamame but meanwhile offered Miss Yoshida a serving of grilled deep-fried tofu with soy sauce and flavoring that was in the 'fridge.

"Do you think you could talk normally?" I asked her. "You're giving me the creeps with all this polite language."

"Okay," she said, sitting down and crossing her legs boyishly.

It occurred to me then that I didn't even know Miss Yoshida's given name. When we were asked to introduce ourselves at the university orientation day most of the girls and a few of the boys turned on their public persona and did the really cute thing. "Umm," said one girl, "I'm Takahashi Mami. Mami is written with the characters for beautiful linen. Make sure," she added coquettishly, "that you read my name characters as Mami and not Asami." Miss Yoshida, however, just said, "I'm Yoshida." That was okay then, but now I wanted to know her full name. When

I asked, she replied, "It's Hanako." So that's what we called her. "If we put both our names together," I said, "they mean 'Peach Flower.'" Later, I called her house once when she was out and discovered that "Hanako" wasn't her real name. Her father, who was very curt and unfriendly, answered the phone. "Who is it?" he grunted gruffly. Being as polite as I could, I introduced myself as one of his daughter's classmates from college. "Would it please be possible for me to speak to Hanako," I asked. "Hanako?" he replied. "There's no one here by that name." Then he slammed the phone down right in my ear. "What's wrong with that silly old goat?" I asked my aunt angrily. I did an impersonation of his disgusting behavior. "Maybe they've just had an argument," was all she had to say on the matter. The next day at school, I spoke to Hanako.

"What on earth's the matter with that father of yours?" I grumbled.

She cursed under her breath. "How many times do I have to tell that man?" she said angrily.

I thought she meant his phone manner, but then she said in a rage, "He never understands. I've been telling that stupid man that I *am* Hanako."

"What do you mean?" I asked, as all sorts of possibilities ran through my head, like maybe this "father" was her mother's second husband or something.

"It's quite simple," said Hanako. "I bloody well hate the name my father gave me so I gave myself a new name but my father won't accept it and gets furious when someone calls me Hanako."

"I see," I said. "But what's your real name? I need to know— otherwise there'll be trouble when I ring."

"Right. Have you heard the famous saying by Confucius, or someone like that, about the body and hair and skin?"

"Nope. What is it?"

"Well it's a sort of moral saying that goes something like

you shouldn't damage your body, hair or skin, or have tattoos or plastic surgery because the flesh of your body is something your parents give you; but my father goes even further to include personal names and claims that we shouldn't ever change the names given to us by our parents."

"That's a bit feudal, isn't it?"

"Yep," said Hanako. That's exactly what it is."

"Well," I said, "lots of anthropologists say it's quite well known that there are many cultures which believe that names have magic powers so they think that it's bad luck to call someone by their real name. And Le Guin actually mentions this too in *The Wizard of Earthsea*, so you could always tell your father that you've become a member of one of those cultures and then you can say you're too scared to utter your real name because of its magic power."

"I suppose I could," said Hanako with a deep sigh. Then after several meandering excuses, she reluctantly resolved at last to tell me her real name. "It's not my fault it's so unsophisticated," she warned, reminding me of someone from an ethnic group that's never had contact with the civilized world and who decides to tell their real name secretly as a token of trust and friendship towards a newfound companion. A bit like the young Iroquois girl in *Triste Tropiques* who comes shyly up to Levi-Strauss to whisper her real name in his ear—although, of course, Hanako wasn't half as sweet as that girl was supposed to be.

"It's Arisa, adapted from Alissa!" she yelled as fast as she could.

"Oh no, that's awful," I agreed.

"It's hideous, isn't it?" said Hanako.

"So I suppose," I said, "the characters in Arisa must be the 'a' in East Asia Air Lines, the 'ri' from reason and the 'sa' from Sagojō—in Chinese they say Sha Wujing—in *Monkey*. If you used those characters to make Asari, like a little shellfish, it wouldn't be so bad. Your Dad must like André Gide," I went on. "What bad taste he has."

"You're quite right," Hanako nodded in agreement. "He does like Gide. I've never read Gide, of course. But when I passed the first stage but failed the second stage of the national university exams for the last two years in a row, I said to my old man, 'Strait was the gate and Alissa couldn't pass.'"

"Did he laugh when you said that?" I asked.

"No way," said Hanako. "He just said something like, oh well, you did your best."

She only told me all this later on. But from the first day she came to visit we called her Hanako or Hana-chan. And that's what we've called her since.

Each Sunday evening Mom would phone and say, "How's everything going? Are you behaving yourself?" This question had a number of meanings. When I'd been preparing for my entrance exams, it had meant first of all that I should be studying. But after I became a college student she didn't worry too much about my studies. What she then meant were things like whether or not I was letting my dirty laundry pile up, or whether or not my room was in a dreadful mess. "I hope you're not taking after your aunt and sleeping in till midday. And don't go indulging yourself in alcohol with that girl." The girl she was referring to was my aunt. "Remember that your aunt is already an adult" (in other words, my aunt earned her own money) "so she can drink beer or wine in the evening. But that doesn't mean you can be drinking with her. And don't think that because she stays up late you can go wandering around enjoying yourself and then coming home late. Remember, I won't have you being slovenly about things." I knew very well what all this meant so she didn't actually need to explain any further. But every time she told me to behave myself, she would elaborate on each of the points listed above. Eventually I would get a chance to ask how things were at home. "They're the same as usual," she'd reply. "I've still got a bad neck and shoulders. Jun'ichi's studying hard. He works much harder than you ever did, you know." Her inane comments would always make me angry and I'd end up crossly asking her to put my grandmother on.

In many ways, Grandma and I got on very well. But it seemed she certainly didn't always see eye to eye with her daughters. "How're things going? Is Chieko behaving herself?" my grandmother would say, lowering her voice over the phone even though there was no way my aunt could hear her. "Look after her for me, will you, and tell her not to smoke or drink too much," she would say. "By the way, I've bought you a lovely summer sweater with green and off-white stripes." My grandmother would then chat on about the presents she had for me. "I've got a few other things here I could send with the sweater—there's some ginger in plum vinegar, a bottle of little pickled plums, a bit of dried fish, and some lovely *wakame*—and I've also got some sheets and summer blankets that were given to me as a return gift from a wedding or a funeral I went to—but you probably can't really wear the summer sweater now so maybe it's okay to wait till you come home in the summer holidays and wear it then."

"Thanks, Grandma," I said, "but I think we already have enough sheets and summer blankets."

"Oh no," said my aunt. "She's sent us enough sheets and towels to last ten years." Then Grandma said, "Put me onto Chieko, will you?"

I handed the phone over. "No," said my aunt, "don't send anything else. We've got enough to last ten years. I'm not a squirrel or an ant. Storing things away makes me neither rich nor happy. You mean for Momoko? But you've already given her about five years worth of sheets and blankets." My aunt was starting to sound a little short. "Okay then, see you later. Yes, yes, you look after yourself too," she said as she hung up the phone. She gave a heavy sigh. "Since you've arrived, your grandmother and your mother have to make a big fuss about everything. But that's okay," said my aunt.

The fact that every day I just sort of hung around doing nothing was partly because university classes were so boring but also perhaps because of my aunt's influence. Right from the time of the orientation, I realized that I had little in common with my classmates so it was all a bit of a bother to talk to them and, besides, I'm a fairly shy person. In both middle and high schools, you might almost have said that I had school phobia because I only attended the minimum possible number of days to get through. In hindsight, maybe I was suffering from mild depression. Anyway, my whole body felt lethargic, right to the tips of my fingers, so that even moving about was a nuisance and all I wanted to do was sleep. That's how things were.

There was an eccentric cameraman called Kobayashi Natsuyuki who often visited my aunt's house. I'd only met him a couple of times but I completely agreed with what he had to say about lethargy. He told us that, for some reason, a few years ago he essentially couldn't get rid of the feeling that there was a thin membrane of skin between himself and the world, as if the existence of things and people had sort of dissolved and destabilized his relationship with the outer environment. He didn't respond to stimuli, like air or wind, on his skin—whether soft or sharp—feeling instead as if his whole body was wrapped in plastic film and that he was sinking under the weight of his own existence. "Can you take photos when you feel like that?" I asked. "Of course not," Natsuyuki replied. "Naturally I don't feel like photographing anything when I'm in that condition."

Although I felt different to how I had in the past, I still had a kind of mild discomfort that made me feel lethargic—maybe, to use a cliché, I had May syndrome—but this wasn't really surprising since, after all, I lived with an aunt who claimed to be in deep depression from her mid-life crisis and problems with menopause, and who spent her time checking the life histories of writers and poets from the past, feeling either cheerful or miserable depending on what these men and women were doing and writing when they were about the same age as her. When you live with a person who, although she complains she can't sleep, in fact sleeps about ten hours a day, you find it impossible not to follow her example—even if you suffer from neither mid-life crisis nor menopause. They say yawning is infectious but I think that sleep, too, is infectious and before long I was also sleeping all the time, just like my aunt.

My mother's calls continued to come regularly each Sunday evening.

"Of course I'm okay," I would always say. "Yes, I've settled in." But in fact, I wasn't studying or doing anything much else either.

I did, however, go to the movies with Hanako fairly often and we also went to book shops and sat around in coffee shops.

"You go to the movies a lot," I said to Hanako, "but you don't seem to have a boyfriend."

"Well," she said, "I sort of do. But boys are boring."

"They are, aren't they?" I had to agree with her. "And it's not just young men either, because, from what I see when editors come to visit my aunt, middle-aged men can also be pretty boring—they say such stupid things—but you ought to see how my aunt reacts," I told her. "She just looks straight past them with a sour face."

"That's exactly what she should do," said Hanako. "By the way, talking about middle-aged men, didn't you say your father is a hotel manager? Do you think," she began gruffly in her usual tough-boy voice, "you could introduce me to him so I could get a part-time job at his hotel in the summer vacation?"

"I think that summer is the off-season," I said.

"You're probably right," she said in a disappointed voice.

"But I'll phone him and ask anyway," I promised.

Since I'm not all that social I'd never really wanted a part-time job, but after two months it had become clear that the allowance of 40,000 yen my mother sent each month was barely enough to make ends meet. Each month she also sent 60,000 yen by bank transfer to my aunt—20,000 for rent and 40,000 for food—breakfast and supper, so to speak.

"Do you think what you send really covers all my costs?" I asked my mother.

"It's more than enough," she said. "Preparing a meal for two rather than one is much more economical, so in fact we're helping your aunt out. Her novels don't really sell all that well, you know."

"Well then, you should pay her more, shouldn't you?" I asked, infuriating my mother.

"You don't know what you're talking about," she snapped.

Out of my monthly 40,000 yen I had to buy lunch, my clothes, my books and things like records; so, in other words, the money had to cover absolutely everything, and although this was okay if I didn't want any clothes, you never knew when you'd see something and think, "I *really* want that." I wasn't sure whether or not 40,000 a month was enough to meet the needs of the average university student, but, for example, when Hanako and I went to see William Dieterle's *September Affair* in Ogikubo, it was 240 yen one way on the Tozai Subway Line from Takadanobaba to Ogikubo, and then, even though it was in a backwater like Ogikubo, they had the cheek to charge 1,500 yen for admission, which was the same as a city cinema would charge for a first release. So a return trip on the train and the cinema ticket alone came to 1,980 yen, which is about the same price as a fifty percent acrylic sweater at a discount store bargain sale. On top of this, we normally had a cup of tea at Takadanobaba, and then, if we were a bit hungry and had something like a sandwich or a pizza, it would soon cost 3,000 yen—oh, and I forgot to say the movie program cost 300 yen. So, when you added it all up, going to see a movie became quite exorbitant. Mind you, in my case I hardly spent anything for books because, since my aunt was a writer, there were plenty of books lying about in her apartment for me to read—although, of course, someone else's books are never the same as your own. But, because I'm a young woman living in a big city where material desires are constantly stimulated, it isn't just books I need—even though I sleep most of the time—and there are days when I feel pretty frustrated both materially and mentally.

Anyway, something interesting happened while we were at the cinema in Ogikubo. Although I've said before that young men are very boring, when we went to see *September Affair* we ended up becoming quite friendly with a couple of self-opinionated boys who fancied themselves as movie buffs. My grandmother collects old feature film videos, so I know quite a lot about movies and while Hanako and I were sitting on a sofa in the cinema foyer, I told her about *Portrait of Jennie*, another movie by William Dieterle, the director of *September Affair*. But as I was talking, I realized that there were a couple of boys listening in on our conversation who were looking quite annoyed. Boys of that age who go to the cinema can be really irritating—you know the type I mean—the ones that look at you condescendingly as if they're worried you'll contaminate the air in the theatre and as if to say they know that you are just an empty-headed girl who reads nothing but adolescent magazines; and if you dare to go and see anything by Godard, there they are, sitting in the front row, glancing at you as they launch into meaningful discussion about film theory and the history of film.

The boys we made friends with weren't quite as bad as that and they certainly attended to their personal hygiene more carefully than many of the boys who sit in the front or second row of art-house cinemas. I remember once reading an article by Hasumi Shigehiko in which he complained about the disgusting body odor of the apparently mindless girls who were at a Matsuda Seiko film and insisted that everyone should have a shower and spray themselves with eau de cologne before going to the cinema. On the whole I probably agree with him, although I must say that I would find a *man* who reeked of eau de cologne completely unbearable, and while I don't actually use perfume, I do think girls should use deodorized napkins or tampons when they're having a period. The point is, however, that young women are not the only ones who smell because, in fact, art-house cinemas and places like Athénée Français and The Film Center are full of boys and young men who go days without washing and who never do their hair so that it becomes one big tangled mess, divided in two and stuck to the backs of their heads as if they've just gotten out of bed. Hasumi Shigehiko should think of a few words to say about these young men as well. In summer, it's even worse, of course, because some of them smell so bad then that your nose and eyes water like you've eaten too much hot chili.

Hanako had spent an extra year studying between school and university but, even so, she barely looked as old as a high school student and could easily have passed as a middle schooler. In fact, to speak more bluntly, she was just like a middle school boy. Certainly, when she talked she used the same sort of speech as a tough adolescent boy and her voice, which was strangely husky, could also go into a falsetto sometimes, just like a boy whose voice is changing. It was this extraordinary voice of hers that gave her a certain unisex appeal and this wasn't just my opinion for, in fact, my aunt also thought Hanako was cute. Mind you, since every time Hanako visited us she made it clear what a great fan she was of my aunt's writing, you probably couldn't rely on my aunt for an objective opinion. I was quite impressed by Hanako's performance, although I did think she went a bit overboard when she once recited a whole passage from memory from one of my aunt's novels. Living the solitary life of the novelist that she does, my aunt is quick to label someone with that sort of dedication to her cause as "sweet" or "cute."

I have to say I was thankful that it was my aunt and not my uncle that Hanako was interested in because it would have been insufferable to have had a thirty-eight-year-old uncle who tried to seduce young girl fans who happened to be my classmates. "That certainly would be appalling," agreed my aunt. "It would be just like the plot of one of those poorly written, trashy post-war *Matinée poetique* novels. But seriously, Hanako is really quite cultured, unlike most girls these days. And, of course," my aunt added, "she has very good taste." When I thought about all this, it occurred to me that I might just like to become an editor of a literary journal myself. I had a few connections which, to some extent anyway, would probably have stood me in good stead; but, more importantly, it seemed to me that all you needed to do to make a writer happy was simply to let them know you had read her or his novels thoroughly—this became obvious when, as she hung up after a telephone conversation with an editor, my aunt said she would happily write if only she could find an editor like Hana-chan. "You mean you don't want to write unless your editor is a fan?" I asked. She smiled slyly and replied. "All the person has to do is to pretend to be a fan. I don't think that's asking too much. It's quite a modest demand, really, but it would certainly make me keep to my deadlines."

Maybe I was being too much of an optimist and I probably had no idea what was really involved, but I thought that I, too, could do that sort of thing and therefore could quite easily become an editor; so I decided that next time my mother or father asked about my future I would say that I wanted to be an editor with a publishing company. This would surely make them happy—both Mom and Dad.

But to get back to the Ogikubo Odeon Theatre, where they pocketed 1,500 yen from adults and 1,300 from students for first-release movies even though it was only just a little nicer than the Pearl Cinema, and, to add insult to injury as if the price wasn't already too much, you had to buy your ticket from a vending machine, something we complained about to a film critic who came to visit my aunt. Anyway, there Hanako and I were, chatting away in the cinema foyer. Now, there aren't all that many people who know William Dieterle's *Portrait of Jennie* but when I told her the plot of the film, Hanako said, "I know that story. I read the comic book version by Mizuno Hideko when I was little." Her response made me a bit annoyed. "Well, I read that too," I said, "but it was plagiarized. Did you know that Mizuno Hideko also plagiarized *Sabrina Fair*?" "Yes," said Hanako almost shouting. "That was so obvious. It was called *The Beautiful Cora*. It was terrible." When she talked at the top of her voice she sounded even more like a boy. "Shhh," I said, trying to make her talk more quietly. "Actually," I went on, authoritatively, "*Portrait of Jennie* was one of Buñuel's favorite films. He talks about it in his autobiography."

"That's right," said Hanako. "Your aunt also cited it as one of her ten favorite movies for a special film edition of the magazine, *Subaru*. It was also listed in the *Marie Claire* ten best film dramas." One of the two boys who were listening in on our conversation from a nearby seat took out a book from his backpack and opened it. Hanako had a quick glance, poked me in the side and said loudly, although I'm sure she thought she was whispering, "Hey, look. That boy over there is reading a book by your aunt."

Obviously annoyed, the boy with the book glared at Hanako who, far from being put off, glared back and said, "What's the matter with you? The book that you're reading was written by her aunt. So don't go glaring at me." She then took a cigarette out of her pocket and lit it with her Felix the Cat lighter, after which she blew smoke all over the two boys, both of whom were starting to look shocked and a little scared. "There's no need to start a fight," I said, trying to calm her down. The boys looked on blankly and made no response other than a stupid sounding, "Right." Still looking rather cautiously at Hanako, they pointed to the collection of film essays one of them had been reading and said to me disbelievingly, "Is she really your aunt?"

"Of course," said Hanako, as if this was general knowledge. I found it all pretty embarrassing, although there wasn't much I could do. Eventually, when the movie ended, the boys (who were, I might add, both over twenty) invited us to drink tea with them at a place near Ogikubo Station. The conversation began on a fairly low key with the standard, "So, you like movies, do you?" But for the following two hours or so we expended all our youthful exuberance displaying the depth of our cinematographic knowledge. Since it would have been a terrible loss of face if the boys had let themselves be outdone by a couple of girls from a private university who were barely older than the adolescent readers of magazines like *Olive*, they quickly got down to serious business, and if Hanako and I had been more experienced we'd probably have just dismissed these boys and their overly earnest conversation as "cute," but, instead, we worked hard drawing on all our knowledge to compete with them and, as a result, ended up pretty exhausted.

"*The Spirit of the Beehive* is a good movie." This was the boys' opening gambit. "I prefer *La Paloma*," countered Hanako. "That's because you have no cinematographic memory of the John Ford western," the boys declared patronizingly. "Well," replied Hanako, "in *La Paloma* there's a part where Peter Kern and Ingrid Caven look at each other through binoculars. Kurosawa Kiyoshi said in an interview that this scene was infinitely cinematographic. And you don't need a wilderness to make a western. Anyway," said Hanako as a parting shot before she left for the toilet, "people are always looking at each other through binoculars in John Ford westerns."

"That younger brother of yours sure knows a lot for someone in middle school," said one of the boys after she'd gone.

"Or maybe he's in high school," said the other.

It took me a few seconds before I realized who they were talking about, after which I burst out laughing because, even though they'd been talking to Hanako for an hour or so, these boys hadn't yet worked out that she was a girl. It occurred to me not to bother disturbing their ignorance but when I changed my mind and told them that she wasn't a boy, they were completely dumbfounded and then panicked and, turning profusely apologetic, begged me not to tell Hanako. "She talks like a boy and she looks so young ..." they said, looking quite crestfallen and deflated.

While I was falling about laughing, Hanako came back. "What's so funny? I could hear you in the toilet," she said accusingly, completely disregarding the fact that her own voice drowned out all other sound. "Nothing, nothing," said the young men, trying to make sure there was no further discussion on the matter. They looked ill at ease and were obviously worried that she may have heard their gaffe. "It sounds as though you're talking about me," she said, standing her ground. "They thought you were my little brother," I told her. "How stupid is that," Hanako said contemptuously. "We don't look a bit alike. If you can't even spot physiognomical similarities and differences, then there's not much point in watching movies, is there?" "Physio-what?" asked the shorter and chubbier of the two, trying to understand what Hanako had said. "P-h-y-s-i-o-g-n-o-m-i-c-a-l. Physiognomical—a person's face." She carefully spelled out the word and its meaning, adding for good measure, "You illiterate idiot."

So that was how we were invited to take part in a discussion group connected to the small private journal that the two boys published on film criticism. The young men were mainly interested in my "brother"—although it's probably more accurate to say they felt threatened by, rather than interested in, Hanako—but I got to go along to the group, too. They also made a point of saying that they would send a copy of the journal to my aunt.

My aunt thought the whole incident was hilarious and laughed out loud when I told her what had happened. "Next time Hanako comes I'll give her a record of the theme-song from the movie *I Even Met the Happy Gypsies.*" She found a copy of the jacket and showed me the feature photo of a little gypsy boy in a hunting cap and tatty sweater with a cigarette butt in his mouth, his grubby face smeared with mud and set in a solemn-looking, grown-up frown. "Don't you think he looks like Hanako?" my aunt asked. "He certainly does," I laughed. "Hanako will love it."

"You know," said my aunt, "even today, if you go somewhere like Wakkanai or those sorts of places in Hokkaido, you can still see small children smoking. They even have Ainu dogs pulling carts just like in the Ouida story, *A Dog of Flanders.* I love that story. It always makes me cry."

"Hang on," I said, getting a bit annoyed. "Hasn't anyone told you that you're being discriminatory talking about Hokkaido like that as if it's some remote place in the boondocks? Just because you saw a dog pull a cart there once doesn't mean that happens everywhere in Hokkaido, you know."

"I always get emotional when I see working dogs or small children smoking," my aunt continued, rambling a little, as I suddenly realized that perhaps I was jealous of Hanako who was clearly a favorite of my aunt. It might sound a bit modernist, but it seems only natural to me to analyze things from the point of view of psychology. You have to remember that my parents divorced when I was a child and I grew up in a family where all my mother's interest was directed towards my younger brother. So it occurred to me that maybe I just craved affection.

7

Things went on as usual with me just filling in time. We sat some incredibly juvenile exams, the low level of which was almost an insult, and although the rest of the class protested about how difficult these tests were, both Hanako and I had a bit of general knowledge to draw on so we found the whole process pretty childish. And, unlike everyone else in the class, we didn't complain about how terrible or difficult the summer holiday assignment was that an enthusiastic young English teacher gave us; in fact, we were rather happy at being asked to compare and contrast Tokyo or Edo, as it appears in a novel from any era, with a city depicted in a novel by Henry James, Edgar Allan Poe, T.S. Eliot or Henry Miller.

Once the groans of "I wouldn't have a clue" had died down around the room, Hanako asked, "Do we have to choose an expatriate American writer?" The teacher smiled and said, "I hadn't mentioned it so I'm glad you realized that all the writers I've given you today are ones who left America." Rather than being pleased, Hanako seemed almost offended at this public recognition.

"So," she continued, "it's okay, then, if we choose a European or South American author writing about an American city?"

"That would be an interesting approach," replied the teacher. "You're Miss Yoshida, aren't you? Which writers were you thinking of?"

"Evelyn Waugh, for instance, or Manuel Puig."

"It's good to see that you've read so much," said the teacher. "Do you have any Japanese writers in mind?"

"I haven't thought about that yet," replied Hanako.

Everyone in the class was clearly impressed by this highbrow exchange between Hanako and the teacher and the other students began to look at her with new respect, including, unfortunately, a girl called Takahashi Makiko who—and I'm sure you've met those girls—had looked, spoken and acted like a middle-aged woman from the moment she was born. This girl now set Hanako and me in her sights as people she wanted to know.

Both Makiko's parents were Christian graduates of St. Paul's College, and since her father was particularly proud of the fact that he'd been in the same class as Nagashima, the famous baseball player and coach, I made a point of telling her one of the many Nagashima jokes I'd heard from a friend of my aunt. According to this anecdote, one day when Nagashima was having lunch in the St. Paul's College refectory, he saw the student beside him consulting a French-Japanese dictionary. "What's that?" Nagashima asked, having never seen a book like that before. "It's a French-Japanese dictionary," the person beside him replied. "When you look up a French word you don't know, it gives you the meaning in Japanese." "That's very helpful," said Nagashima. "I wish I could get one of those with the Japanese meaning written in English." It was quite a well-known joke but when I told the middle-aged Makiko she was seriously taken aback. "Is that true?" she asked in amazement. "Is Nagashima really that stupid?" And this was the girl who now spent all her time talking to Hanako and me and who was determined to be our friend.

"That was great, Miss Yoshida," she said following Hanako's classroom performance. "You really impressed Professor Nakano. You're full of insides, aren't you?" Now what Makiko had actually intended to say was that Hanako was good at making "insights." But her pronunciation was so bad (she'd probably never used the word before) it ended up sounding like "insides." This is certainly what Hanako heard. "Full of insides? What are you talking about? I haven't got a beer gut," Hanako retorted.

Only momentarily puzzled by Hanako's response, Makiko

continued unfazed. "Do you think I could come next time you two go to the movies? And I wonder if you could give me some help with my English literature essay?" She then turned to me and said, "Your aunt's a novelist, isn't she? So she'll probably help with your essay, won't she?"

I had long felt uneasy about the idea of women who did things in threes because, regardless of their age, they were rarely the sorts of women you could call beautiful, although there were some exceptions, for example, among older film stars and other fading popular culture icons—and, of course, there were also the three court ladies in the Girl's Day doll setting. Hanako and I, therefore, were doing our best to avoid Makiko and were luckily helped by the fact that the summer holidays arrived, so when she said to us, "We have a house in Chigasaki. Why don't you come and visit during the summer?" we were both able to decline indirectly but nonetheless legitimately. "I'm going back home to the country," I said. "I'm busy with my part-time job," Hanako said. However, a complication of a different sort arose.

Hanako had asked me to introduce her to my Dad who, as I had imagined, responded to my request with the usual lecture. "I won't be giving her any special treatment just because she's a classmate of yours, you know," he said. "But okay, why don't we have lunch together and then I can ask her a few questions. It's a shame," he concluded ramblingly, "that you only think to ring me when you want to ask me something." This last comment referred to the tension in the personal relationship between my father and me and I frankly have to say that I don't like him very much—for that matter, I don't like my mother either because all I really have in common with either of them is the fact that they are my parents. If they weren't, I doubt I'd have anything to do with them.

Anyway, Hanako passed the informal job interview and we had lunch with Dad. "What would you like?" he asked. "How about tempura? Isn't there a tempura restaurant in this hotel?"

I replied. "There is," he said, "but it's not so good." With that, he took us to Yanagibashi, where we had tempura in a perfectly traditional Japanese room by the river where an elderly man in a white chef's uniform sat formally on the tatami matting beside us. "Please permit me to deep-fry your tempura," he said as he began to prepare our meal. I'd been there before, but because it was Hanako's first time she was pretty stunned and it was all she could do not to laugh at that sort of ritual. Afterwards she said, "It was great fun, wasn't it? It was like we were foreigners or guests from overseas. We should have spoken in English."

But this wasn't the problem I was going to tell you about.

Now, the job my father gave Hanako was as a waitress with a white apron in the lounge of the hotel. "You'd earn more money as a room attendant," my father said, "but it's physical work and you need to be quite strong. You look very healthy, Hanako, but you're quite small so one of those higher paying jobs is probably not for you. Now if it was Momoko here," he turned to me as he spoke, "she'd even be able to work in a boiler room." This was his feeble attempt at a joke and, although I suppose it's just the sort of thing a middle-aged man would say, it shows how brainless my father is. I wonder if he realizes the negative effect these jokes have on our relationship. As we left, my father gave me 20,000 yen in pocket money. This greatly impressed Hanako. "Your old man is really quite bourgeois, isn't he?" she said. After we left Yanagibashi we went to Roppongi to see *Alpine Fire* at Cine Vivant and then to Takadanobaba to see *Pierrot le Fou* and *Paris Texas*. We also planned to see a Naruse Mikio special showing at the Institute of Dramatic Arts the next day. "Hey, why don't we submit something to the cinema diary section of *Lumière*?" said Hanako suddenly. "Great idea," I said. "We could give ourselves a penname using part of each of our names. What about Momo-hana, the peach flower. Or," I suggested, "we could use the Chinese readings of 'peach' and 'flower' and call ourselves Tōka." Hanako was uncertain about this. "It sounds a bit like a haiku penname," she said. In any case we became quite excited at the prospect of writing something for a film column together and talked for a while longer before going our separate ways home. But in the middle of the night my aunt and I heard a knock at the door and there was Hanako standing on the doorstep telling us she'd left home after having had a fight with her Dad.

"You're very welcome to stay here," said my aunt. "But, while I don't want to sound reactionary, you should probably ring your parents and let them know where you are. After all, you're not an adult yet so you're still really dependent on them."

"I don't want to," said Hanako.

My aunt thought for a moment. "Okay, then," she concluded. "You don't need to ring."

"My Dad usually doesn't come home till late," Hanako explained, "but tonight he was at home, drinking beer and watching a baseball game. You know how some people who come from Tokyo just have to be different and so they follow other teams because they think it's too ordinary to support the Tokyo Giants? Well, my Dad reverses that so even though he wasn't born in Tokyo he thinks it's cool to follow the local Tokyo team. Anyway, Kuwata was pitching and the Giants were winning so I waited till the game was over and then told him about my part-time job. He completely lost it. 'Like hell!' he screamed. 'You're not having any part-time job.'"

"Why ever not?" I asked Hanako.

"Perhaps ... he could be a bit like Yoshimoto Takaaki," said my aunt.

"You're absolutely right," said Hanako. "My Dad just loves Yoshimoto Takaaki."

"Hanako," said my aunt, "what does your Dad do?"

But Hanako went on without answering my aunt's question. "'If you become a waitress,' he ranted, 'then you'll end up working in a no-pants nightclub and the next thing you'll be in a massage parlor.' He was absolutely disgusting. 'What are you talking about?' I yelled back at him. 'They had to make up the Oedipus complex for people like you.' Then Dad screamed at me, 'Don't go throwing the half-baked theories you've read about at me!'" she said.

"Try not to be too upset, Hana-chan," said my aunt. "You have to look at things from your Dad's point of view. He mightn't do it perfectly, but he does support you and pay your tuition fees so that theoretically you don't need to work. And he gives you what he thinks is enough pocket money for a girl at university. What he's probably trying to tell you is that even though we live in a society where everyone's desire for material goods is being continually aroused, it's wrong to try and satisfy these in a way that's going to jeopardize your fundamental obligation as a student—which of course is studying—by trying to get a job to earn some easy money. I think that's probably what he was trying to say." This is pretty much what my aunt said to Hanako although it certainly wasn't what she would have really been thinking.

"I suppose so," said Hanako. "But, like I told him, he hasn't even read *Anti-Oedipus* and he accuses me of throwing half-baked theories around. 'And anyway,' I said to him, 'you spend all your time editing some American-style magazine obsessed with health.' That made him really mad. 'Don't be so smart,' he screamed. 'If you've got any complaints then get out.' So I left," said Hanako, "and here I am."

"Hang on," said my aunt. "Is your Dad an editor?"

"Yeah," said Hanako as if to say, "So what?"

"And your name's Yoshida, isn't it?" asked my aunt. "So you would be Mr. Yoshida's daughter, wouldn't you?" The look on my aunt's face made it clear that she found this rather tricky, and, although I could see that she was being very careful not to let Hanako see her expression, since I had heard a really dreadful story from my aunt about this man I was unfortunately unable to stop myself from blurting out, "Oh no, you're *his* daughter!" How sorry I felt for Hanako who must have been so embarrassed to have had a father like that; although later I would come to have mixed feelings about my own father and I'm not sure which is worse—finding out that your father's a sexual harasser or that he's a homosexual.

My aunt managed to cover up her shock and avoid having to tell Hanako what she meant. I already knew the story about Hanako's Dad. And it wasn't a nice story at all. "Does this often happen?" I asked my aunt when she told me. "I can't really say," she answered. "But since I haven't heard any other stories like this one I don't think there are too many people who are as depraved as he is."

The story went something like this. Hanako's Dad was the chief editor of some new "we all need to be aware of physical fitness"–type magazine called HELP. Anyway, along came some good-looking, young woman photographer—whom some men might have thought at first glance that it wouldn't take too much to seduce even though all she wanted to do was sell her photos to the magazine. So the chief editor, who was Hanako's father, told her she had a good photographic eye and suggested that, if she had no other plans, they should have dinner together. Now, it was a bit hard for her to say no because, not only did she want the job, but Hanako's father was your typical authoritarian middle-aged man who used to be in the radical anti-Yoyogi faction of Zengakuren during the sixties student movement. (I knew his voice from talking to him on the phone and he sounded exactly like *that* sort of middle-aged man.) It never occurred to the young woman photographer that he would ever say to her, as he did, "I'll give you a job if you sleep with me." She simply thought that, being a fellow journalist, it'd be worthwhile for him to know what professional "information" she might have and that he'd be interested to find out about recent developments in the photography world; anyway, she seemed to believe that this dinner would just be a work-related exchange between an editor and a photographer.

Now the idea that it's okay for a man to expect sex from someone he asks to dinner might be the type of classic sexist myth that circulates in places like New York or Paris, but I can assure you that most of the editors that I'd seen at my aunt's place were desperate for information rather than sex. Whether they'd read the material themselves I wasn't sure, but they were always bringing my aunt first issues of new magazines and newly published novels by young writers and trying to save themselves work and get easy access to information by asking her opinion. Anyway, to get back to the woman photographer—who'd been a junior student at the photography school my aunt's friend, Natsuyuki, went to—my aunt said that she'd been so angry that she'd written a letter of complaint to the publisher. Apparently, she'd asked Natsuyuki what he thought she should do and was pretty annoyed when he told her that there were these sorts of men out there in the world, that she should just think of them as being a bit sex-crazed, and that it would be best to leave things as they were, ignore what had happened and look for work somewhere else. After telling Natsuyuki she wouldn't have thought he was so conservative, she slammed the door and marched out. "I suppose I should be glad you didn't say it happened because I'm good-looking," she said as she left. The letter she wrote became a hot topic of conversation among the publishing company staff and, because the magazine always featured a wide selection of photography, also among the magazine photographers' network. All of which meant that Hanako's Dad felt rather uncomfortable about staying in that job so he shifted to another magazine which didn't depend so heavily on photography.

"Have you ever worked with him?" I asked.

"Mm, I did, a long time ago," my aunt laughed. "I was an unknown writer and had written some short stories for his magazine. Later, when we were drinking with some people after a party, he told me that because I was a woman I had to pour the beer and be nice to everyone, but because of the family business I was used to customers who said things like that so I pretended not to hear and just thought instead, 'Shut up, moron.'"

My aunt and I both suddenly remembered this incident at the same time and it made the two of us feel a bit uncomfortable.

"And if your father," said my aunt to Hanako—and you might note that the "Dad" we'd been casually referring to now suddenly became "father"—"is against your working in a hotel, maybe you could work for me, writing clean copies of my manuscripts." Hanako's face lit up immediately. "Well," she said, "I'm very proud of my handwriting. In primary school I even won a gold medal for my calligraphy of 'fresh morning' in the National Mainichi Calligraphy Competition." My aunt's face also lit up. "Did you really? That's great. That's perfect," she said brimming over with happiness. "Of course, I can't pay you too much." In truth, this was a totally unrealistic idea that my aunt had only come up with because she felt sorry for Hanako and wanted to make up for gossiping about her father. I could understand this but my aunt's plan was quite impossible.

"Auntie," I said, "I'm sorry to ask this, but where exactly are the manuscripts you want Hanako to copy?"

"Where are they? I'm going to start them right now."

"But they'll take you months to complete, won't they? When you have to hand in a manuscript to a magazine you always leave it right till the last moment. So there'd be no time for Hanako to make clean copies."

"I'm not talking about magazine articles," my aunt defended herself. "Hanako can help with my book manuscript."

"Your book manuscript?" I asked in amazement. "Auntie, Hana-chan needs a job now and I'm sure it would be terrible if she had to tell Dad, 'Oh sorry, I can't work for you. My father won't let me because of this or that reactionary reason.' You'd hate that, wouldn't you, Hanako?"

"You're right, of course," said my aunt.

Meanwhile, Hanako had a new idea.

"Perhaps," she suggested, "I could stay here. I'll do anything you like. Calligraphy, cooking, cleaning—anything."

Even though it seemed to me that this wasn't such a bad idea, I still thought my aunt should try and persuade Hanako's father to let her work. Of course, without letting Hanako know, what I was really trying to imply to my aunt was that she should blackmail Hanako's father with the gossip she'd heard, but my aunt seemed to be standing firm on some principle she had of not meddling in matters of family discipline.

"But at least," said my aunt, "you can stay here tonight. Will I ring your parents?"

"No, don't!" shouted Hanako.

At that point the phone rang. My aunt picked it up, said hello and then identified herself in a jolly sounding voice. "It's been ages since I've seen you," she said. From her manner it was clear that the caller at the other end was in a bit of a panic and I realized that it must have been Hanako's father. "Your daughter and my niece are in the same class at college. They're great friends. Yes, Hanako's here with us now. No, no. It's no problem at all. We love having her. You have a wonderful daughter. She's certainly a lot more mature and responsible than our Momoko." After a few comments like this, my aunt's tone changed a little. "I heard there was some difficulty at your work," she said with a light-hearted but rather suggestive laugh. "Oh," she went on, "I also hear that Hanako is going to work with my brother-in-law. He is absolutely meticulous, you know, and your daughter seems to have made quite an impression on him. He's even eager to have her on the full-time staff after she graduates. I'm so sorry to keep her here so late. No, not at all, she's very welcome.

Perhaps she could even stay here tonight. Shall I put her on?"

Apparently, all Hanako's father said to her was, "You can take that part-time job," and then hung up immediately.

"We won, we won!" we shouted. "This is fantastic. Let's have a beer," I said. "Damn," said my aunt. "I've run out of beer." She sounded like it was a major catastrophe. "No problem," said Hanako, who had come over to our place on her bicycle, knapsack on her back. "I'll jump on the bike and go and grab some from a vending machine."

In the end, both Hanako and I rode down to the liquor store on Mejiro Street where we had a bit of an argument over whether to get a mini-keg or ordinary cans with a selection of plain lager, draft and stout.

"Just because you're small you want the great big one."

"But a mini-keg looks so cool."

"It's actually very un-cool."

"But you feel like you're really drinking beer when it comes out of a keg."

"Yeah, but I want to drink some stout as well."

We rode home through the beautifully moist evening along the deserted street filled with the fragrance of late climbing roses, gardenia and four o'clocks, our faces cutting through the evening breeze as we raced along to see who was the fastest. Small drops of condensation covered the cans clattering in the baskets attached to the fronts of the bikes so that when we arrived home and opened them foam spurted everywhere and we all grinned happily for no reason in particular. "I'm going to buy you both a present with the money I get from my part-time job," said Hanako. My aunt smiled and turned to me. "Will you look for work in the holidays, too, Momoko?" she asked. "Well, maybe," I replied uncertainly, unable to give a clear answer as I slapped at and squashed a mosquito that had landed on my arm. "Actually," I said after lighting a mosquito coil, "I think I'll take it easy this summer."

And I did. I went back home and spent most days of a very lazy and relaxed summer either watching my grandmother's video collection or reading books, and, when occasionally I was seized by a kind of inexplicable irritation, I would take my bike and ride at top speed along the beach. I also helped Grandmother pick the corn growing in the back yard which she'd planted with hopes of an abundant harvest. But most cobs had barely any kernels. And sometimes I just slept on and off all day. Since my empty holiday time was filled with those sorts of boring activities, in the end I put on two kilos and became rather depressed, and, although Hanako wrote to me every ten days or so, there wasn't much in her letters but, more than that, her handwriting was so awful that she must have been telling an outright lie when she said she'd won a gold medal in the Mainichi Calligraphy Competition—or perhaps writing with a brush is completely different to writing with a ball-point pen.

At the end of September my father had a car accident. We found out when my aunt took a phone call from Dad's partner. "Apparently he'll be in hospital for three months or so, so you should probably go and see him," my aunt said to me. "Oh well," I thought, "I suppose I should." But there was a shock waiting for me when I arrived at the hospital, for I had absolutely no idea that my Dad was living with a man so, to be honest, I was pretty stunned and came home in a bit of a turmoil. "You and Mom knew, didn't you?" I asked my aunt. "You both knew all about Dad." She did her best to apologize, even though she didn't really need to. "Well, your mother and I ... you and your brother were only children, you know ... there was no way to explain things to you. I'm so sorry." Then she said, "You don't really need to take it too seriously, you know. These things happen in the world."

8

"It's okay for you to say that these things happen in the world," I said. "But this is not out there in the world—this is my father, so of course I'm upset."

"I think I understand how you feel," said my aunt, still trying to find the right thing to say and clearly feeling that, as someone who'd experienced life and as a novelist who'd seen a lot more of the world than her nineteen-year-old niece, it was her duty to give some advice. For a minute or two she looked rather perplexed trying to think of something accommodating to say.

"Look," she began, "I could tell you that you'll understand your Dad's feelings when you are older but since you're unlikely ever to be a male homosexual, that's probably not the case." My aunt gave a hearty laugh. "So the best thing I can say is just to turn a blind eye because people will be people and you can't change that. At first your mother was really hurt and said it was even more insulting than being left for another woman but she's recovered now and, in the end, no one's in a position to comment on anyone else's sex life. It's certainly not something I want to talk about and, anyway, who cares about people's preferences or inclinations? You know, there's nothing abnormal about homosexuality, and, besides, your Dad really loves you."

"Does he just?" I answered. "Well, I don't actually like him all that much." Then I added, "We just don't get on." Anyway, the whole thing began to seem pretty unimportant and even as I listened to my aunt I thought it wasn't worth thinking about anymore. Anyhow, I decided not to tell my mother I knew about Dad—although we really wouldn't have had much opportunity to talk about that sort of thing—and I also decided not to say anything in front of my younger brother, Jun'ichi, until he found out for himself. And so that, I thought, would be the end of the subject.

My aunt seemed strangely despondent and irritated and I was a bit worried that talking about my father might have made her depressed. "Look, this is my problem and I can work it out for myself," I said. "Yes, that's what you have to do," she replied with a sigh after which she stood up cheerlessly and said with a theatrical air, "I was so upset, I had a drink all alone in the middle of the day." She went into the kitchen, took out a large bottle of sake from under the sink and poured herself a glass. "Would you like a glass, too?" she asked. "The line I just quoted is a heart-rending statement of pathos and woe made by Higuchi Ichiyō in a story by Izumi Kyōka—although there's nothing pathos-filled or beautifully heart-rending about how I feel. While you were at home for the holidays, I ... well, after I saw all those special features in the papers and on TV—you know, the ones that they have in August to commemorate the end of the war—I decided to read a book called *Dear General MacArthur*—the Supreme Commander of the Occupation Army in Japan from the end of the war until 1951 was a man called General MacArthur. Oh, I see. You know that? Good on you. Oh, so you've seen Gregory Peck playing him on television, have you? That's right, with a corn-cob pipe in the corner of his mouth. Yes, that's him and, you're right, he's the general who said the Japanese have a mental age of twelve, although, of course, we can't say he was totally wrong there, can we? But, anyway, this book introduces a selection of letters written to MacArthur by people in Japan during the six years that he headed the Occupation. Apparently, there are five hundred thousand altogether, with letter after letter nothing more than a desperate display of sycophancy to this dictatorial leader—it even occurred to me that my own parents might well have written to him," my aunt observed with a sigh.

"And that's not all," she continued. "This summer I read ten or so full-length novels by contemporary Japanese writers and, I can tell you, fiction is well and truly dead, so then I read a few short stories in a couple of literary magazines, but all that did was get rid of both my appetite *and* my sex drive. I'm so depressed," she wailed, slumping down on the couch. "Ahh, why ever did I decide to become a novelist? How terrible things are." She gave another sigh, although, personally, I thought her reaction was a bit extreme.

It occurred to me to tell her to write an essay about how she felt but I stopped myself since I didn't need to hear her tell me that because I wasn't an editor I wouldn't know anything about what she should or shouldn't write.

The next day at university I ran into Takahashi Makiko. "There's something I need to ask you," she said, dragging me off to a quiet place behind the library where no one would see us. "Would you mind saying I'm staying at your place the weekend after next? I need you to ring my parents and tell them I'll be there that Saturday night."

"Sure," I said, "whatever." Though I had absolutely no desire to know why she wanted to lie about staying at someone else's place, it was clear that this was exactly what she was dying to tell me. "And don't say anything to Hanako," she said. At the time I thought she meant that if Hanako knew so would everyone else, but she was probably more worried that Hanako would abuse her for being stupid if she found out what was going on. Anyway, I was pretty annoyed and said to her, "I don't mind ringing your parents but there's no need for you to tell me why you need to spend the weekend away from home." But it was to no avail. "No, no," she said in a teary voice. "I want to tell you." "Please, no," I thought. "I don't want to hear all this." For, to tell the truth, I was sick and tired of hearing about the love lives of other people. Only the day before at a coffee shop near the hospital where Dad was, I'd been forced to listen to a tale of woe from my father's moon-faced, flower-designer lover. "I'm sorry, my dear girl," he'd said weeping. "On top of everything else, I'm sure you'll be shocked to know that your Papa wasn't alone when he had his accident. He was with a young man." Frankly, I was fed up with that sort of conversation.

But to get back to Makiko, she turned out to be something of a dark horse because she told me that she had a boyfriend whom she'd dated since high school and that, for his birthday, she'd given him—quote—the "gift of my virginity." After that, he'd demanded the same gift every time they went out and she'd ended up pregnant. But it taught me that you can't judge a book by its cover since I would have thought—obviously incorrectly—that girls who look like middle-aged women from the time they were born would be better organized in matters of sex and had imagined, for instance, that if their boyfriends didn't use condoms they would only have sex on safe days. Now that she was pregnant, Makiko said, there was nothing for it, of course, but to have an abortion, so she needed to say she was staying with a girlfriend in order to spend a night in hospital. "Is that so?" I said flatly, showing no interest whatsoever. Nevertheless, she started going on and on about her boyfriend, about the sort of person he was, about how they would be married after graduation, about how kind he was and how he had cried with her when she decided to have the abortion, about how the 18-carat gold ring she wore shaped like a ribbon had been the present he'd given her on her birthday, about how his father was the branch manager of a big supermarket, about how her boyfriend lived away from the family by himself, about how his big brother was studying computers in the Graduate School of the Engineering Faculty of Tokyo University and was someone he really looked up to, and how this gave the boyfriend a bit of an inferiority complex, but how, even so, he himself was very smart and studying commerce at Waseda University, about how his mother was a Christian and a graduate of University of the Sacred Heart, Tokyo, and about how she, Makiko, was overjoyed at the thought of having such a woman as her mother-in-law. On and on she droned interminably, her glowing language making her sound like a go-between talking up the virtues of a prospective marriage partner. "Okay, okay. No problem. I'll call your place," I said, doing my best to bring the conversation to a close. "Thanks so much," she said excitedly. "Please make sure you remember," she added with some urgency. I was very tempted to ask, "If you're a Christian should you *really* be having an abortion?" However, since I knew that this would just prolong the conversation, I kept quiet.

The next day Hanako took the day off college so I unfortunately wasn't able to tell her about Makiko, for, although Makiko might have asked me not to tell Hanako, I hadn't actually promised anything. Since as well as asking me to ring her parents, she had forced me to listen to her stupid bragging about her boyfriend, I couldn't wait to tell someone who would sympathize and certainly never thought that telling anyone would be the wrong thing to do.

When I arrived home, my aunt was still depressed and unhappy and had spent the day lying around in her pajamas, only moving occasionally to go to the toilet. Even though she was always like this just before she started to write a novel, looking at her also made me feel quite despondent, so I stayed in my room reading a book. But her gloom gradually infected me too.

When I was studying for my entrance exams, even when I was doing something like laughing out loud at a television comedy show, I'd felt a dark and heavy pressure that had actually never really gone away and the same horrible feeling could well up within me any time I had a problem. I lay on my bed, looking absentmindedly at the ceiling and must have nodded off because suddenly I awoke to find the room in complete darkness and, since the living room was in darkness, too, my aunt must have been in her room asleep. When I looked at the time it was ten o'clock and I was starving. But going to sleep and waking up at such odd hours induced a depressing lethargy in me. Suddenly, however, my aunt appeared. "Is it really ten o'clock?" she asked. "Aren't you hungry? What shall we do? Why don't we go out and get something to eat?" Her voice sounded surprisingly fresh and cheerful. "Right," she called out, trying to organize our outing, "let's have a quick shower. Then we can go to eat *yakiniku* in Shibuya."

The next day my aunt finally started working on the short story she should have been writing for *Gunzō*.

Bringing Up Baby

"I'm pregnant," she said over the phone. Just like that. Nothing else, not even "Hello." Then she said, "And it's your child." She rang early one morning, around seven-thirty. "Who was that?" asked my mother. "One of your friends from exam prep school? Whoever it was, she sounded upset." Mother tried her best to probe my private life with a few obvious questions.

Few men would be overjoyed at this news. None, in fact. Generally they'd be terrified. Certainly, for me, it was like a nightmare. An absolute nightmare. She'd said "child," but she really should have said "fetus," shouldn't she? Naturally, she had to have an abortion; there was no question about it. And, even though it was really an accident, I was quite prepared to take financial responsibility for the unfortunate result of my actions. I wondered if she'd be able to claim the operation on health insurance. Anyway, I decided to get the money somehow. I started at breakfast by telling my mother I needed extra cash for books and things for school. That got me 35,000 yen. I thought I'd try to borrow the rest from my big sister. Then if I needed more, I could always get a bit from a few of my friends who were already in college and who had more time to work part-time and earn money. I thought they'd probably have some cash I could borrow.

Okay, I know that super-reactionary people will think I'm showing a lack of respect for life, but there was, in fact, nothing else for it but to have an abortion. Usually I hate that expression: nothing else for it, even though we'd be kidding ourselves if we really thought that we had any choice in the things that we say or do. But in this case, from where I was sitting, it was clear there was definitely no other choice. At prep school, they're always telling us that there's nothing else for it. Of course they're talking about the need to study to pass the university entrance exam. And my older sister tells me that "nothing else for it" was also a favorite propaganda catch cry of the radical student movement. By the way, my sister's an unmarried mother. She knew our parents would oppose her having a child before marriage so she kept her pregnancy a secret until it was too late for an abortion. She was about six or seven months when she finally came home from her apartment and proudly declared she was having a baby. "I have chosen to have a child," she announced. "Why didn't I tell you sooner? Because I knew you would tell me to get rid of it and have an abortion. And I have no intention of getting rid of my child." If you ask me, she probably didn't even realize she was having a baby until she was five months gone. She was always telling Mom how irregular her periods were. "Well, since you're more than five months, I suppose there's nothing else for it but to have the child." That was my mother's response. So, you see, the phrase "there's nothing else for it" can be used even with a decadent or miserable nuance as in this case of my sister. But I truly believed that, for me, there was no other way. Having a child was just unthinkable. For a start, since we were both doing an extra year's study to get into good universities, neither the girl nor I had any income. But even if I'd been able to support myself, the thought of having a child was just too much.

I have to confess that I find the idea of parenthood pretty awful. When we say "parenthood" we should probably just say "motherhood" because, it seems to me that, as far as the child is concerned, fathers have a pretty meaningless existence. They're just shadows in the background. At best they might become like mothers. But mere shadow or not, I had no desire to turn myself into a parent.

My sister, you know, used to argue much the same thing. She was always going on about how the parent-child bond was even more important than the male-female relationship. She also had this theory that the wife and mother-in-law pair was like a social institution that mimicked but also disguised the tension between mothers and daughters. This was the basis of the graduation thesis she did for her sociology degree before she became an unmarried mother. I'm not sure she was all that serious about her argument. It was more like something she just made up at the time. In the thesis she compared Kurahashi Yumiko's *The Scorpions* and *The Doctor's Wife* by Ariyoshi Sawako, and then talked about a few other novels by women. What an absolute waste of time that thesis was. But, anyway, for a while I thought that my sister really hated motherly things as much as I did. Maybe this just means that I relied on her as a sort of maternal substitute. Yep, perhaps that's what it was. From the psycho-analytical viewpoint, you'd probably say that. It's only common sense, I guess.

But, where was I? Oh, I remember. Maybe I should tell you from the beginning how things had happened. On the phone that morning, Yumeko and I agreed to meet before class. Her name is Satake Yumeko—you know, "yume" for dream. Stupid name, isn't it? Pretty dreadful, really. I've never met them, but I'd say her parents must be a pair of losers. So, anyway, we arranged to meet just outside the station. She'd sounded pretty panicky on the phone and I expected a dramatic scene. I'd like to point out that I'm not completely inhuman. Since I knew the dangers involved and was aware that having an abortion wouldn't really be all that good for her health, I was a bit worried about her. And while I realized that you couldn't just walk in and ask for an abortion at a big public hospital, like the Red Cross Women's or the International Catholic Hospital, I certainly didn't want her ending up in some sleazy, backstreet clinic. I wanted to make sure that she went to a proper hospital and, once again, I hoped that my sister would help. Her boyfriend's a doctor and I thought I'd ask him for the name of a clinic. This was all going through my head on the train as I made my way to meet her. By the way, this doctor boyfriend is totally loathsome. I could just hear him saying, in a macho action comic character voice or like some actor in a television drama, "You might have enjoyed yourself fooling around but the time's come for her to suffer." I wasn't sure I could bear being embarrassed like that. And as for the idea that sex is always so great for men, what a pathetic myth that is. It's on a par with the claim that women have deeper and longer orgasms. Believe me, I didn't have any fun having sex with Yumeko, although I can't exactly blame her for that. But you have to agree, don't you, that the whole process is actually pretty miserable? "Is this all there is?" I thought. And I bet she thought the same, too. "I don't think I like having a penis put in," she said afterwards. "I wonder if that means I'm not physically developed yet. It should be softer," she went on. "I think I just want to pet." But, of course, I wasn't interested in that. It wasn't the first time for me. And I certainly wasn't in love with her. It was just one of those things that happens.

I had run into her during the summer when I went to a live concert of the Southern All Stars. The music really got me going and I was quite excited by the swing of her hips. You know their song, "Your hips make my heart beat." Well, it was exactly like that. Although there were lots of students there, there were also some biker gangs wearing either matching Aloha shirts and shorts or *happi* coats and shorts. The atmosphere was just amazing. The whole thing, to use an expression that's a bit out of date these days, was extremely "laid back." And it was a scorcher of a day. There they were, those bikers, covered in sweat, stomping their feet, clapping their hands and yelling in time to the music. When the concert was over they just went off home in their sandals. Bikers, you know, are fundamentally all conservative, if not totally ultra-right wing. In other words, they're a pack of petty fascists. At the end of the day they all think like Tanaka Kakuei and believe in the same sort of soppy moral code you read about in traditional stories. They mightn't observe the road rules but they certainly obey the "system." I can say this now but, at the time, I longed to be one of them. My own life seemed incredibly boring; so, naturally, I was envious both of them and of all their visible signs of excess.

My brother and his wife in Kyoto had just had a baby and, on the day of the concert, my parents had gone to see their new grandchild. Since I'd been left at home by myself I wanted to eat out and I invited Yumeko to come along too. And, it had been my intention to pay for us both. But then she said, "It's so expensive to eat out. Why don't I cook something for the both of us?" Now there are some men who would appreciate such an offer, and I can't say that I'm entirely innocent in that regard. "You probably can't tell, but I'm quite good at cooking," she told me. "I'm sure you are," I thought. "You look like the type whose specialty is macaroni cheese and cream croquet, with the occasional batch of chocolate cookies thrown in." Many boys would undoubtedly like a girl like that. Some might even go so far as to call her "cute." Well, I made the mistake of having sex with that sort of girl. I can tell you now, I would have been better off with someone who had given me a dose of the clap. I really would.

I admit I only have myself to blame for not using a condom. But you'd think a girl would know that she had a good chance of getting pregnant if she had sex at a certain time after her period, wouldn't you? Mind you, I only got all the information about things like ovulation days, birth control and pregnancy from the *Home Doctor* after she told me she was having a baby. So I'm not really in a position to point the finger. But, unreasonable though it may have been, I was angry with her. Okay, I know that's selfish, but you have to remember that I didn't actually get to do anything enjoyable.

When I talked to my sister, the unmarried mother, she exploded. According to her, it was arrant male egoism to tell a woman to have an abortion. Well, maybe she was right there, but what do you think about what she said next? "Even when a woman decides herself to have an abortion," my sister announced, "she really wants the man to tell her he wants her to have the baby. The fact is," she continued, "and this is something that only a woman with a child can understand, women actually want to give birth and have children. No woman really wants to have an abortion. It's true, the girl you made pregnant is still preparing for university and so are you. So I understand that you can't possibly raise a child—and no one knows better than I how unbelievably difficult it is to work and to raise a child alone. I agree that there's nothing else for it but to have an abortion." As she spoke these words, the "unmarried mother" handed me a pamphlet. "Here," she said, "you'd better sign up with this organization. It's a group that's fighting changes to birth control legislation that will make abortion more difficult." The pamphlet was a tract on women's independence, but it also had a lot of stuff about the value of maternity and read a bit like some mother-child melodrama. "Anyway," she gave me a final volley, "I think it's pathetic that all you can think about is getting rid of the inconvenient little creature created by your sexual indiscretions."

In spite of this sermon, I did manage to borrow some money from my sister and to get an introduction to a doctor. "Make sure you pay it all back," she said. "I'm not here to fund your sex drive. And don't you forget that I'm a single mother." Although I was relieved to have the funds, I still had to find a way to make sure that Yumeko agreed with my plan. She certainly seemed to want to have an abortion. "I'm a woman so I'd like to have a child," she told me when we met to discuss the details, "but right now I can't," she said, doing her best to force a few tears to run down her cheeks. She talked as if it was an accepted fact that every woman wanted a child. This really irritated me so, even though I knew I was being juvenile, I said to her, "No one is born of their own volition." She looked blank. "You know," I explained, "that's what kids always say when they argue with their parents—that they didn't ask to be born. It's absolutely true." Of course most parents want to give their kid a clout when they hear that. They are pretty knocked about by this cold hard truth. In fact, it's quite a mean thing to say.

> Yumeko: It's a bit childish to talk like that, isn't it?
> Me: Of course it is. That's because it's children who say it. Parents don't ever say that sort of thing.
> Yumeko: Don't be so juvenile. You sound like you're in junior high. Besides, parents having children is what life is all about. Aren't you glad you were born?

Unfortunately, my smart comments didn't have the desired effect. But since it wasn't me having the abortion, I felt I couldn't just tell her to calm down. That would have been pretty irresponsible given that she was understandably fearful and uneasy about the operation. She also felt quite guilty about having such a procedure, although I doubt she felt guilty about having sex. The fact that she was pretty scared made her face look stressed-out and dark. In fact, she looked awful, as if she wasn't getting enough sleep. Then she started telling me about some folklore researcher she'd read who wrote about the god of dead fetuses. This researcher had some pretty predictable things to say about women forced by poverty to abort their children with no other resort but to pray to this god. "But," Yumeko wailed, "he said that these days young women just go off, have the operation, and kill their children without a second thought." Reactionary clown. "Maybe he's a follower of the Seichō no Ie movement," I said.

Yumeko: Seichō no Ie? What's that?
Me: It's a religious group. Haven't you heard
of it?

I showed her my sister's pamphlet which, because I'm a bit stupid, I thought might make her feel better. In fact, it had precisely the opposite effect. For in the pamphlet my older sister, the "unmarried mother," had written a lengthy essay on abortion guilt. "While it may be a logical error to regard abortion as a sin," the pamphlet claimed, "nothing can erase the guilt and sadness of a woman who loses her child this way." Yumeko was clearly very pleased to be feeling so miserable when she read this. "That's right. A man could never understand," she declared. Then she continued reading. "Whether or not," wrote the "unmarried mother," "the fetus has a personality is of no consequence to the feeling of a woman who has a child growing inside her." Now, if you change the word "fetus" in this passage to "child," namely the child the mother gives birth to, then you start to get some idea of how the mother defines herself. In other words, she doesn't actually care about the personality of her child. I heard they have machines these days that can measure the unborn child's heartbeat and their growth rate. Mothers are overjoyed when they see the child's heart beating on the monitor or the shadowy form of the child inside them moving about. It's said that mothers feel this joy because they believe that the growth of the living body within them is some sort of infinite mystery. It makes the pregnant woman feel that the fetus is part of her own life.

And it's not just the unborn fetus that mothers regard as part of themselves. Believe me. I can tell from the attitude of both the "unmarried mother" and my own mother that they actually think that the children they give birth to are an extension of, at the very least, their own selves. Sometimes the "unmarried mother" puts on a show that her own child is an eerie amorphous Other—no wonder, given the theme of her graduation thesis. But let me quote you some extracts from her pamphlet: "A pregnant woman regards the fetus as part of her own life, and hence, ..." (sorry to interrupt here, but I really have to point out that this use of "hence" is a huge jump in logic), "... hence," the "unmarried mother" said, "to discard this part ..." (when she says "this part," what she really means is the bit that is part of her), "... regardless of what natural scientists might say ..." (in other words, it's a question of what you think the words "person" and "the self" mean), "... discarding this part can bring nothing but sadness." She went on to claim that asserting the right to have access to an abortion leads to a guilt-ridden darkness. The pamphlet also made a range of other righteous claims referring to things like the pill and why it was wrong to take advantage of women's guilty feelings by calling abortion "murder."

Yumeko nodded her head in agreement over and over. "Yes, yes, that's absolutely right," she said. "I would love to meet your big sister and have a talk. She's such a brave woman." When I then said it was my sister who recommended the abortion and lent me the money, Yumeko had no compunction in saying, "But we can't help it." I was a bit concerned that she spoke in the plural like that. Even though human beings distinguish between sex and reproduction, these occasionally become the same thing. Since I had to think of some sort of solution, I decided to have a vasectomy. This might either have been a defense mechanism or just my narcissistic impulses, for I didn't really have too much sympathy for women who have abortions, and neither did I feel responsible as the man. It was simply that I just did not want to become a parent. Absolutely no way. You might remember the folklorist that Yumeko was talking about. This guy talked as if the person who kills the fetus is necessarily the woman. However, a friend of my brother who was a cultural anthropologist at the University of California took some LSD—

he said it was for a scientific experiment—and hallucinated that his Navajo Indian girlfriend, who was also his research assistant, had conceived a devil. So he stabbed her with a knife and ended up murdering both the fetus and his lover. He knew that his girlfriend was pregnant and now he's in Sing Sing Prison. Some people sure are fearful of having a child.

So, anyway, Yumeko had the abortion. While she was hospitalized she told her family that she was staying at our place. It was quite a conscientious hospital so the procedure required a two-night stay. The gynecologist boyfriend of "the unmarried mother" insisted that, since I was the father of the fetus, I should go and visit her every day. He also told me to wait at the hospital while she had the operation. "You should witness her suffering," he declared. What a hypocrite. But I couldn't actually refuse. "Okay," I said. There was really nothing else to say.

Trite though it might sound, I'd had a bad dream the night before. In the dream Yumeko told me she was determined to have the baby and so I ended up stabbing her. It was terrifying. However, when they wheeled her out of the operating theatre in a wheelchair, her face was clear and bright. In fact, she looked as fresh as a daisy.

> Yumeko: That wasn't as bad as I thought it would be.
> Me: ...

It sounded as though she'd just had a tooth pulled. I had no idea what to say. Later, the "unmarried mother" said, "Oh well, one of these days, she'll become a mother and then she'll have a child and raise it. But there's nothing else for it this time." Anyway, at least Yumeko didn't fret too much about everything, which was a relief. After she had the abortion, though, and was lying in bed in her hospital ward, she did start sniveling, "I've lost my baby." For some reason it was now "my" baby, not "ours," which I thought was a bit presumptuous. "You'd better not get too emotional," I said. "You'll upset yourself." I really wanted to tell her not to be so sentimental but I kept myself under control. But she looked pretty distressed and ended up bursting into tears. The other patients in the ward were middle-aged women and they snuck glances at us that clearly said how immoral the young people of today are. "If you can't have a baby, you should be using birth control," said the looks on their faces. "And it's always the woman who has to bear the pain." But I actually hear that most women who have abortions are married. Besides, what's the difference between an abortion and birth control anyway? Theoretically they both end up with the same result—no baby. That, of course, is if we leave out the physical risk involved.

I didn't actually say all this to Yumeko. But some time later, at a party for people who managed to pass their exams and get into college, she got really drunk and started rambling. "I can't help feeling I destroyed a life," she kept saying. So that's when I told her what I thought.

But she wouldn't listen. "This exam victory came at the price of the life of my child," she wailed instead. She behaves very badly when she's had a few drinks and it's not just the alcohol but because she's actually a bit stupid. It seemed to me that she was, in fact, proud of having had an abortion. Maybe it made her feel like a fully fledged, independent woman. The look on her face said, "I'm different from those other immature girls."

As well as that, the bloody "unmarried mother" told my mother everything, but Mom, in fact, seemed pretty unfazed. "Well," she said, "when girls these days have an abortion they just take it in their stride. You told me she passed the entrance exam without any problem, didn't you? She must be very strong, don't you think?"

And that's the whole story. Eventually there was no need for me to have the vasectomy because, ever since then, I've been impotent, although I suppose you don't really want to hear about that. I've heard that this is a depressingly common story. But it seems to me that this sort of consequence is a bit predictable, like something straight out of a psychology textbook. For, in fact, the real culprit is the formula that says pregnancy equals being a mother, which is just all too vulgar and ordinary.♋

* * *

As I read the story after it came out the following month in *Gunzō*, I thought it was a bit strange that my aunt found it so difficult to write this sort of light-hearted, entertaining piece. When I finished reading, I told my aunt, among other things, that a girl who spends an extra year studying to get into a national university wouldn't speak like Yumeko does in the story. "Can't you see there's a moral here," she replied calmly. "Girls who speak to men in a way that is different from the way they speak when they're with other girls always end up having an abortion."

It was clear she wasn't really interested in hearing what I had to say.

9

Soon it was November, and one of those days they call an "Indian summer." It also happened to be my twentieth birthday. My aunt and I had been invited to a party to celebrate my father's recovery and Hanako was invited too, not so much because my father himself had taken a fancy to Hanako but because my father's partner and Hanako had hit it off the minute they met. That's how she was invited.

"Your father helped me get a job so I should probably go and see him while he's in the hospital," Hanako mused after Dad had his accident. "Why don't you come with me?" she asked, leaving me with little choice but to go along to the hospital too. "What do you think we should take him?" she pondered. "Do you think he'd like a book? A pocket book mystery should be okay, shouldn't it?" I was a bit hesitant. "I don't know whether or not he reads books," I said. Hanako thought again. "Maybe you're right," she said. "If my father's any example, then middle-aged men don't read books, do they? All they seem able to manage is a magazine. But, your father's in hospital so he's probably really bored. What else could he do but read?" So we decided to take him a few books. I have a writer aunt and Hanako has an editor father, both of whom are always being sent complimentary copies of new books from publishers and authors, so we took a couple of these from Hanako's father who, since he never reads anything anyway, was hardly likely to miss them. And because my aunt always puts the books she doesn't want in a big pile, I just took a few from there and that way it ended up costing us nothing. Hanako even told me that she occasionally took a few of her Dad's books and sold them to make a bit of extra pocket money.

When we arrived at the hospital, Dad's partner, whose name

was Kaidō, was there too and, although Dad had given me no explanation about his relationship, he acted now as if I knew what was going on and should approve of the situation as a fait accompli. He seemed to assume that Kaidō had already told me what I needed to know. As far as Dad was concerned, the fact that I had come to see him with a friend was a sign of my acceptance of things and he was, therefore, very happy to see me. So was Kaidō, who made a cup of Fauchon apple tea for both Hanako and me and then offered us some Godiva chocolates.

Even though I had heard that this apple tea was one of the most popular Fauchon products in Japan, it had an artificial, ostentatious, sickly taste that neither my aunt nor I liked, while Hanako really hated it.

"The French must have something wrong with their noses, don't you think?" I said. "People are always giving each other this terrible stuff. They come to your house and bring it as a gift and then you wonder what to do with it so you give it to a friend who knows it's expensive but can't drink it because it stinks so much and then they give it to someone else, and, the next thing you know, it comes back to the person who gave it out in the first place."

"Goodness me, young lady," said Kaidō archly, "what a wicked little thing you are. But I adore this lovely *thé* made from *pomme*. And your Papa loves it too." Hanako had never heard such camp speech before (neither had I until I met Kaidō) and she was absolutely fascinated.

Following this exchange the hospital room became quite lively. Hanako was in a great mood and I also felt very positive and laughed obligingly whenever Kaidō made a silly joke. Eventually Dad asked Kaidō to take us out for a meal and after we ate Chinese in the Ginza, the three of us went to a gay bar in Shinjuku.

So that was how Hanako met Kaidō. Probably because the party we went to was being held to celebrate Dad's recovery, no one remembered my birthday and, anyway, turning twenty and becoming an adult wasn't actually all that important to me. But since it did seem to be a good opportunity to get a present for myself, I announced to the gathering, "By the way, everyone, it's my twentieth birthday." Dad immediately went into a spin and ordered another bottle of champagne. "Okay," he said, "let's have another toast." This was the first time that I'd ever drunk champagne, and it was so cold and delicious that, although my life had a number of complications, the world seemed serene and peaceful as it floated beautifully before me.

I held the glass against the light of a candle and looked at the champagne bubbling palely amber. "If only I could spend my whole life doing nothing except drinking champagne like this," I said to no one in particular. "But, my dear," observed Kaidō, "you have no memories in your glass—you should always drink champagne with memories of passionate love," he continued. "Some people," said my aunt, "are like Uchida Hyakken and they just like champagne—Hyakken was drinking champagne from a straw just before he died." Then she turned to me, suddenly remembering my reading tastes. "You've just turned twenty," she said. "What are you doing reading writers like Uchida Hyakken? You should be reading books written for young people. You're not old enough to have such subtle taste." I was quite surprised by this outburst but later that night, something of a catastrophe occurred when, after dinner, we went to a small piano bar in Roppongi where the young man who was with my father at the time of his accident turned up. Apparently he and his love-sick heart had been searching everywhere for my Dad and, now, having finally found his goal, the young man came over to our table rather abruptly. "I need to talk to you," he said in a strained voice as he gazed at my father with bloodshot eyes, totally oblivious to the presence of the rest of us. "Well then," said Kaidō, "it's easy to see that you're going to ignore *me* completely." His gestures and intonation were decidedly camp. "Young ladies," he said, with an exaggerated flounce, much like Tamasaburō might have given in *Nihonbashi*, "it seems it would be better if I excused myself." My father gave a fleeting sideways glance at Kaidō and simply said, "Yes, that's probably best." Kaidō replied, "I'll be waiting at home." I felt really sorry for him and was so ashamed to be my stupid father's daughter. The atmosphere at the table was now distinctly tense and cloying. "Well, we'll be going now, too," said my aunt. "Okay, then," said Dad. "I'm sorry the evening has ended like this," he added apologetically.

Since then I haven't seen my Dad so I've no idea what happened after we left. But, just as I was beginning to think that none of this had anything to do with me anyway, there was a phone call from Kaidō. "I know it's not much use telling all this to you, my dear," he began, "but I've let your Papa know that I will never leave him. A younger man might well be more attractive. But, then," he wept, "what did these last fourteen years mean?" My aunt took the phone from me and made lots of sympathetic noises.

Perhaps because the warm days were dragging on, I simply didn't feel like going to university and spent my days lying in the sun, napping. "This is just like having a cat in the house," my aunt said, rather taken aback at first at my languor. But soon she started to get a bit cross. Hanako had recently been spending a lot of time with her boyfriend and seemed to be quite enjoying herself. My mother, on the other hand, spent her time complaining about the downturn in the family business. "It's not a hot springs resort, you see," she explained grumblingly.

Since I didn't feel like doing anything except eating, and since everything tasted good, I ended up putting on three kilos and even had difficulty fastening my skirt; but, while on the one hand this was a problem, on the other hand I didn't really care. That was how I felt.

"There's no sky in Tokyo," said Takamura Chieko, according to the famous poem her husband Kōtarō wrote. But if you're lying at a sunny window on the fifth floor looking out at the clear autumn sky laced with wispy clouds, your spirits feel pleasantly sleepy and your mind becomes somehow blank; and when the sun warms your body, making you feel a bit itchy you know that all you need to do is to stretch your arm around to scratch your back and, as Browning once said, "All's right with the world!" And though there's nothing particularly wonderful happening, you can't help smiling and stretching contentedly as you roll over on the floor. It seemed to be my rolling around that particularly irritated my aunt. "You look like a tuna flopping about like that," she complained. "Can't you try to be a bit more active?" She said this even though she herself slept all day and spent her evenings reading in bed.

I wondered if it was okay to live like this, but then immediately thought, "Why not?" as I drifted off to sleep.

It was on a day like this that my aunt said, "I think I'll go on a trip." And she went out and bought herself a great big suitcase.

10

~

"I need a change of scene," said my aunt. "I'm not looking for anything dramatic but I'm tired of the monotony of everyday life—they say that eighty percent of American women who are closet drinkers were driven to alcohol because they couldn't stand their monotonous lives."

"Do you really have a monotonous life?" I asked watching my aunt stroke the shiny leather of her brand new suitcase. "It's not really that bad, is it?"

"It is rather," said my aunt. "I'm not a great Romanticist, you know, but I can't bear the thought of spending all my time from now on doing the same thing: earnestly writing novels." Then she added, "Not that there's anything much wrong with that— and I suppose I could regard living with you as something of a change of scene."

After this, my aunt said she had a number of manuscripts to write and set to work very conscientiously. "So she *can* do it when she puts her mind to it," I thought to myself. After writing four essays and a short story over two nights, she put them in separate brown paper envelopes and wrote on each the name of the magazine in which they would appear. "Make sure you don't mix them up when you give them to the people who come to collect them," she said.

The essays went to *La Mer*, *The Monthly Kadokawa*, *Quarterly Letter-writing*, and the Monthly Bulletin of the *Iwanami Philosophy Lecture Series*. The short story appeared in a PR magazine.

Look-alikes

I occasionally walk down Mejiro Road to the shopping centre in the Commerce Complex in front of Mejiro station. Mejiro is not very convenient for everyday shopping because the Peacock Store and the grocery section in the basement of the Commerce Complex are the only places to buy fresh produce. Since market forces like to take advantage of a lack of competition, the fish and vegetable prices there are two or three times higher than at the Nagasaki Market which is quite a way further down Mejiro Road.

Certainly, none of this is anything that girls are interested in. As Akutagawa Ryūnosuke famously suggested in one of his short stories, once a girl starts to worry about the price of vegetables we can no longer call her a girl.

It makes me very annoyed to pay 50 to 70 yen for a bunch of Japanese basil at the Peacock Store or the Commerce basement grocery department when I can get ten bunches for 200 yen at the Nagasaki greengrocer. However, this is not the place to make a comparison between the respective prices of the shops in Mejiro and those down the road at the Nagasaki Market. I'll save that for another essay.

The Commerce Shopping Complex is just beside the Kawamura Girls' Academy. Since the Peacock Store is closed each Tuesday, if I want to shop on Tuesdays I have to go to the Commerce Complex. When I do, I often run into crowds of well-fed junior and senior high students on their way home from the Kawamura girls' school.

When I went to school, students who weren't very clever tended to go to private schools that had very strict dress and hair codes.

Kawamura Academy also seems quite rigid in this respect because its students, who tend to be round and plump, wear their long hair pulled back into plaits.

Now I'm not trying to establish whether or not there's a connection between school rules and academic ability. What I want to say is that, from the way these girls walk, they could easily be mistaken for middle-aged women on their way to the shops.

Women who've reached middle-age often feel the need to confirm their existence by riding their bicycles, loaded with shopping bags and the odd child or two, straight down the middle of the pavement. They aggressively ring their bicycle bells as if to say, "Here I come, get out of my way." Or, they walk unbelievably slowly. Furthermore, they are rarely alone, but rather move about in groups of three or four. Perhaps they meet at the food section of a store, where they stand about and chat for a while. Then, they leave the store and, since they are all heading in the same direction, dawdle down the street side by side, taking up the entire footpath while children the size of brown cockroaches yell and scream around them.

The extremely slow walk of these women is exactly the same as the walk of the school girls from the Kawamura Academy. In fact, if you remove the herd of brown cockroaches and replace the shopping bag with a school bag, there is no difference whatsoever. Given their mass, we might use the word "hammer" rather than walk. However, since this can give an impression of speed, perhaps "thud" is even better.

If mode of walking is the sole criterion then it is impossible to distinguish between girls and middle-aged women. Furthermore, if we assume that gait reflects attitude to things in general, then the girls from the Kawamura Academy have at least in spirit already reached middle-age. Similarly, if we want some insights into the thoughts of the middle-aged woman, even a quick glance at the magazines they read makes it clear that these women are essentially still girls. For, if you examine the types of articles written in magazines for girls and magazines for middle-aged women, you'll soon see that apart from a few extra things, like the advantages of investing in mid-term bonds or the signs and symptoms of menopause and the problems of old age, there is very little difference. In other words, middle-aged women are still very much girls.

Therefore, there's no need for middle-aged women to privilege their girlhood. Neither should girls be contemptuous of middle-aged women.

The only difference between the two is that middle-aged women

look slightly older.

That is all there is, which is perfectly obvious to everyone except the girls and middle-aged women themselves.

There is one other similarity, namely irregular periods. Since girls have just started menstruating they can have irregular periods while middle-aged women are at the end of their reproductive cycle and can also have irregular periods. Middle-aged women tell girls, "Everything will settle down once you're married. I was like that." Similarly, older women say to middle-aged women, "It's great when your periods stop. I was like that." ♋

Even the President Changes Every Four Years

What do you say to the lover you decide to leave after four years?

In Suzuki Seijun's *Muteppō Taishō* (The Big Boss Who Needs No Gun), Yamaoka Hisano is the mother of high school student Wada Kōji. Since it is a 1961 film, Wada is young enough to carry off this role. Now, there is a scene in which Tomita Chūjirō, Yamaoka's lover and bar-owning employer, tells her she's lost both her job as the mama of his bar and her place in his bed. This news comes out of the blue, with Tomita making a statement to the effect of, "From tomorrow another woman will run the bar." Then he adds something like, "And you're no longer my moll." As a specialist villain with a distinctive bad-guy face, Tomita delivers this line with suitable cold-heartedness. Yamaoka Hisano, of course, is shocked by the news. She begs him to reconsider, pleading, "But we've been together for four years." Now, obviously, being someone's lover and running his bar for four years is no guarantee that this situation will last forever. So Yamaoka's plea is actually meaningless, although we tend to say meaningless things all the time.

> Hisano: But we've been together for four years.
> Chūjirō: Even the President changes every four years.

What does Yamaoka Hisano then do? In response to Tomita Chūjirō's rather futile line she merely looks stunned, draws in her breath and remains silent.

I don't think I need to explain why I find this scene so

hilarious. Whenever my friends and I discuss films by Suzuki Seijun, I always perform these lines, although no one else seems to be as impressed by this scene as I am. Furthermore, whenever there's a presidential election in the United States, I always hear Tomita Chūjirō's voice saying, "Even the president changes every four years."

For the words of a lover, this line is notable for the absence of any frisson of kindness. Nevertheless, it was probably the best thing in terms of keeping the other party quiet and persuading her to make the necessary break. If someone told you this, you'd be unlikely either to argue for the possibility of a second term or to point out that the French President's term of office is, in fact, seven years.

In this sense, it's a great line that silences everyone completely. We might therefore say that it's just like the writing of Ishikawa Jun. ♋

Dear Letters

Perhaps you've already heard that some people are known as "letter vampires." While the average person, of course, doesn't turn into a vampire merely by writing a letter, we could label Kafka and Proust as "letter vampires" and also, perhaps, Flaubert. Occasionally, I read back over the letters of Kafka and Flaubert, although it's not something I do for fun. It's rather that, as a professional writer—an occupation which I must concede is somewhat contrary to the times in which we live—and let's remember that none of the three writers mentioned above was a writer by occupation—I am sometimes tormented by an irritating lethargy. When this happens, I somehow feel a longing to read the letters written by these "vampires."

Whether it is a plain white page or beautiful sheet of quality paper featuring various elaborate strategies designed to convey one's profound good taste and social humility, to gaze as a writer at the blank space that has not yet, but that will, become a letter is to feel a sense of anxiety. Of course, the letter-writer can fill the page with whatever words and thoughts she or he might chose. Nevertheless, as these words appear on the page, accompanied by the awkward scrape of a pen being pushed across paper, it can be difficult to decide whether the letter is indeed being written to the "Dear" recipient who bears the name given on the envelope above the address and the postcode, or, in fact, to someone else. This may be why the writer makes every effort to inscribe the sign of his "Dear" recipient in sentences such as "Do you know what I'm thinking now? I'm thinking of the sweet little slipper enfolding the tip of your slender little foot." Nevertheless, although the woman who receives the letter does perhaps wear the "sweet little slipper" referred to, the rose-colored satin might be much more tattered than the writer imagines, while the decorative fur pompoms can be covered in dust like the coat of a cat on heat endlessly out on the prowl.

Emma, in fact, will eventually wear the same slippers in the room of a sleazy, garish hotel room in Rouen, while the heroines of other novels will dangle slippers from the tips of their feet thirty years later in a Venice hotel or a hundred years later in a Berlin boarding house.

But I think we digress. When I read this slipper letter, I recall a sentence from Nabokov's autobiography. "Happy is the novelist," writes Nabokov, "who manages to preserve an actual love letter that he received when he was young within a work of fiction, embedded in it like a clean bullet in flabby flesh and quite secure there, among spurious lives."

Well, my dear letters, would you wish to be embedded like this in a novel? How would you feel at such a fate, you that are constructed from words and the particular way that writers grip their pens, the instability of their feelings and memories, their secrets and sighs, and the paper and ink that they so carefully select.

Long ago I wrote a series of "you" addressed to a certain name, which I probably did because, just as Gilles Deleuze observed, "you" yourself are a vampire. Having said this, I am sure that Nabokov's words suggest a better hiding-place for a letter than the common card-rack which the famous detective, Dupin, brilliantly revealed. But, when you think about it, to whom do "you" really belong? To the writer or to the recipient?
♋

Text and Texture

Even those who know nothing about semiotics are, of course, still able to watch movies and read novels and poetry. Whenever I finish reading a book on semiotics, I immediately forget what it was about. So when I hear Roland Barthes referred to as a semiotician it is difficult to imagine that this could be the same person who authored the several thin volumes I occasionally re-read for pleasure.

Being a novelist, I feel no obligation to remember anything about books such as the Japanese translation of the laborious work of Gérard Genette. Nor do I feel it necessary to feign that I am too aloof to read works like this. By the way, whenever I hear the name Genette, I always think of white hawthorn because I once mistook the French word *genet* to mean hawthorn rather than Scotch broom. I was quite interested in this writer's *Discourse of the Novel*, although, while they don't appear all that often, the lists and tables he uses, such as the four combinations of person and narrative categories, are, frankly, rather off-putting. In contrast, Roland Barthes's *The Fashion System*, a work I find rather boring, has numerous lists scattered throughout, although perhaps "numerous" is an exaggeration. The lists in this work, however, give the impression of being arranged so that, rather than having to engage in semiotic analysis, the reader might enjoy the texture of the relevant signs.

This is partly because the signs in question are costumes—or, to be more accurate, representations of costumes, whose surfaces are generally highly tactile—and partly because the epigraphs heading each chapter are a series of quotes taken from fashion magazines. These reveal the longing of

Barthes, the whispering voice whose breath is heard, too, in the fragments scattered throughout the later works, including those beautifully slim books, *A Lover's Discourse*, *Pleasure of the Text*, *Roland Barthes / by Roland Barthes*, and *Camera Lucida*. The Barthesian sigh that caresses the sign is never heard in Genette.

Perhaps it is true that, as Barthes says, we fail to talk about the things we love. It may be precisely the reason that I open Barthes's books, and other books, too. That is, I long to share the writer's sad pleasure of loving something and failing to talk about that something. Moreover, we read for the pleasure of remembering. "A leather belt, with a rose stuck in it, worn above the waist, on a soft Shetland dress." "A little braid given elegance." "A cotton dress with red and white checks." "Gauze, organza, voile, and cotton muslin, summer is here."* These epigraphs from *The Fashion System* permit Barthes to convey the richness of the "variants of configuration" (and what a bizarre term this is!) of the language of fashion. Reading these words, the reader has a sense of fabric being sensitively and pleasurably cut and then sewn together with typical Barthesian brilliance. It is also in this book that Barthes provides evidence supporting the claim that the words "text" and "texture" derive from the same etymological source.

Barthes's last book was *Camera Lucida*. In this work, a color Polaroid by Daniel Boudinet operates as an epigraph. It is a photograph, not surprisingly, of fabric; everything visible is tinged with blue, the foreground featuring an object like a bed or divan on which lies a rounded cushion made from the same fabric as the divan cover. Immediately behind is a window covered by a curtain through which enter rays of bright light. The curtain is blue and made from a worn fabric

---

* Translators' note: These epigraphs are quoted from Richard Howard's translation of Barthes's *The Fashion System*, London: Jonathan Cape, 1985, pp. 3, 27, 71, and 100.

marked by the occasional tear, roughly woven from thread with a strong twist that could be wool muslin or cotton. Both the stitching line and the area where the drapes overlap are dark blue. Between the drapes is a tiny opening shaped like a long triangle. It is a "bright room."[†] The one layer of blue curtain fabric, woven with substance, but also soft and transparent, permits light to penetrate while shutting out the bright white rays of the sun which undoubtedly abound outside. The brightness of the light stains the upper section of the curtain like a flame which consumes and thus enters the openings made by the warp and weft of the fabric (Antonin Artaud). In this way, the cloth becomes a transparent membrane through which the liquefied light can pass. The slight fullness of the drapes and the curve of the stitching suggest that a soft breeze blows through the open window into the room. What appears to be a horizontal trace across the fabric, a shadow that transverses the curtain, creates the impression of the balcony rail on a terrace outside the window. My intention in giving a description of the photograph used to illustrate the book is not, in fact, to highlight the various relationships between text and texture suggested by this image. I simply want to say how much I love the slim little work entitled *Camera Lucida*.

This is because I feel that I may have read the book somewhere in the past. It was, in fact, in something I wrote myself. Narcissistic though it may sound, in 1971, long before I read *Camera Lucida*, I wrote a short story about photography entitled "Windows."[‡] When I read back over sections of my own writing, and it is tempting to quote parallel passages

---

† Translators' note: Hanawa Hikaru's Japanese translation of Barthes's work is titled *Akarui heya* (Misuzu Shobō, 1985), which is the direct translation of *La chamber Claire*, the title of the original.

‡ Translators' note: Kanai Mieko's short story "Mado" was published in 1976 rather than 1971, and formed a part of her omnibus novel, *Tangoshū*, Chikuma Shobō, 1979 (translated by Paul McCarthy as *The Word Book*, Dalkey Archive Press, 2009).

from both books although this would prove nothing and only embarrass me, I cannot help but feel that I wrote this piece after reading the text by Barthes. However, *Camera Lucida* was written in 1980 and in 1971 it would have been impossible to read a book written nine years later. Besides, the narrator of my story, "Windows," does not have the deep affection Barthes had for his mother.

> Hence the Winter Garden Photograph, however pale, is for me the treasury of rays which emanated from my mother as a girl, from her hair, her skin, her dress, her gaze, *on that day*.
>
> (*Camera Lucida*)§

> The first time I saw my mother's face was in a single photo I possess. It was also the first time I experienced the strange and melancholic solitude of childhood. But what made me even more unsettled was the light that surrounded this already non-existent mother. The light in this photo surrounded a girl who was as yet unmarried and to whom it had never occurred that she might one day have a son. Whatever became of this light?
>
> ("Windows")

The other decisive difference between the two texts is the fulsome "treasury of rays" in the Barthes text and the paucity of the extinguishing light in my own. We always try to analyze the

---

§ Translators' note: Richard Howard's translation of Barthes *Camera Lucida* (Hill and Wang, 1981, p. 82) is used for this quotation, with the change of "child" to "girl" to reflect the Japanese translation by Hanawa Hikaru to which Kanai refers.

unsettling feelings evoked when we look at an old photo. While we might describe this by using the "other tune" called "pathos," the passage I wrote is better described using the Barthesian term, "forlorn." ⁵

Could it be that I am a reader, and a writer too, who, despicable in my bourgeois complacency, reads in books only those things that I can understand. ♋

⸹ Translators' note: *yorube no nasa* is the phrase used in Satō Nobuo's translation, *Kare jishin ni yoru Roran Baruto*, p. 29, for *détress* (distress). The nuance of the Japanese expression, however, is closer to "forlorn" than "distress."

Flower Tales

Onēsama came into the garden through the wicker gate leading from the road. She wore an *ōshima* fabric kimono with a matching *haori* jacket, the fine pattern of which was almost like the cloth used in a man's plain kimono. Her glossy *hakata* obi with its black pattern on white background was held in place by a tie-dyed pale blue obi scarf featuring white snowflakes and a fine flat scarlet obi cord tied slightly on the diagonal around the lower part of the obi band. A dusky rose pink cashmere shawl lay across her shoulders. Unaware of my gaze from the window, she stood before the sasanqua camellia hedge at the edge of the pond staring momentarily at something I couldn't make out.

I was about to call to her, "It's cold. Won't you please come on inside." However, I refrained, for she looked so slender and beautiful that I longed to gaze at her a little longer.

Beyond the slim branches of the weeping cherry tree and the willow that grew in front of the pond, the water's rippling surface reflected on the fair-skinned face she had partially hidden by pulling her shawl up closely with both hands. Has she not done this, her entire face would undoubtedly have shone pale and white.

"She's probably choosing some sasanqua cuttings for her ikebana," I thought and decided to tell her of a friend's garden where the sasanquas were much finer than those in our own. Conscious though I was that I should boil some water to make tea for a guest visiting on such a cold day, I was unable to tear myself away from the window. As Onēsama took several steps towards the stepping-stones encircling the pond, her hem fluttered back in a circular motion revealing the pale blue lining of her kimono. For an instant I spied the dark navy straps of her *zōri* making a clear geometric shape across her white *tabi* socks. She took a small jump and landed lightly on one of the stepping stones that lay where the water was quite shallow about a meter out from the edge of the pond. She then leapt effortlessly across the gap of seventy centimeters or so which lay between this and the next stone. Whether because the wind was blowing or purely from the movement of her body, as she landed, both arms outstretched, her rose pink shawl slipped from her shoulders and floated down to land gently on the surface of the water. The shawl was then swept by the wind out of reach across the pond where it lay on top of the water like a piece of the elaborately decorated, long rectangular Japanese paper used for writing poetry.

Slipping into my sandals I ran from the verandah, flustered. As I did, Onēsama saw me and said in a soft, tender voice that held no hint of disquiet, "I need a stick or something. You can't reach from that side, can you?" While she watched me racing here and there looking for a stick, she crossed to my side of the pond by the stepping stones. "I wonder," she said, "if there's something in the shed." By then, however, I'd waded into the pond wearing my sandals. The cold water was at first only ankle deep but soon my calves and then the fronts and backs of my knees were also immersed. I stretched out my hand to the edge of the cashmere shawl and scooped it up from the surface of the pond. Since the fabric appeared to be water resistant, the shawl had remained relatively dry. Instead, the soft furry cloth was covered with numerous small moist droplets, as if sprayed with tiny beads. There were also several darker stains that marked where the water had, indeed, soaked into the fabric. When I shook the shawl the water droplets dispersed, accompanied by the faint aroma of perfume.

"Look! Mission accomplished." I called. "You silly young lady," said Onēsama. "Hurry up quickly now and come on out of the pond. Quickly," she said once more, stretching her hand out to mine. Wrapping the shawl around my neck I made my way towards her outstretched hand through the ankle deep mud and collection of dead leaves that lay at the bottom of the pond. As we grasped each other's hands I realized that hers was rather large for a woman so that, in spite of the soft, long elegant fingers, it had something of an androgynous air about it. A flesh-colored band-aid was wrapped around the tip of the middle finger. Her cold fingers and palm encircled my own and held my hand tightly as I balanced myself with my foot against the stone edge of the pond.

"You're soaking wet, aren't you?" said Onēsama. "The hem of your skirt and slip are drenched and your socks are all muddy." I held my skirt and slip together with both hands and wrung them out. Then I washed the mud from my woolen socks by dipping my feet and splashing them about one at a time in the water of the pond. "Oh dear," laughed Onēsama. "How careless you are. Take those socks off or your feet will freeze."

She made me lean against the stone lantern beside the sasanqua where, after removing each sock with her cold fingers, she held them together and wrung out the water. "Perhaps they'll shrink," she murmured. Then, turning back to me she said, "Your feet are like ice. Look how red they are." With that she took hold of my foot and dislodged the wet shreds of blue wool lint from between my first and second toes. "What a tomboy you are," she laughed.

I was fifteen and it was a weekday morning. Realizing that the winter holidays had not yet started, Onēsama asked why I was not at school. "I stayed at home because I've got a bit of a cold," I replied. "Oh dear," she said widening her eyes with concern. "Let's go inside and get you warm." She gave me a hug. "We can have some hot cocoa."

For some reason there was no one else at home except for the old housekeeper so we spent the day alone until the family returned late in the afternoon. My father was master of the ikebana school that Onēsama attended and I assumed that she had come by hoping he would be here to discuss the one-woman exhibition she would soon hold.

"Why didn't you ring before you came?" I asked. "And why come today? No one should be here."

"Yes," she replied, "I should have rung. But when I was on the train I somehow just felt like coming here. I wanted to see your face, Haruna."

"Really? Is that true?" I asked. "But I'm usually at school and wouldn't be here."

"I would have been happy to wait," said Onēsama.

"But you're so busy."

"Even when you're busy," she said, "you can still, as they say, find a quiet moment."

This was the sort of innocent nonsense the two of us exchanged.

"Now then, why don't I cook you something," suggested Onēsama. And so we ate macaroni and cheese. Although she prepared some salty water in which I heated my feet after coming out of the pond, this didn't stop my cold from developing. It had been a rather inadequate excuse for missing school, but as we ate I found that I couldn't stop myself sneezing. My nose was running and my eyes were watering too. I took my temperature to find it was about thirty-seven point five.

"You'd better take some medicine and go to bed," said Onēsama.

"It's too boring going to bed alone," I cried. "I couldn't bear that."

"Alright then," she said. "I'll read you a book."

I explained all this to my male companion as we walked along together. "The pond was just there, in front of where the house used to be and where the Ikebana Hall now stands," I said. The house opposite had not changed at all and so I knew this was where I had lived as a girl. Thinking of the beautiful woman I'd called "Onēsama," I realized that I had been in love with her.

While I might have been fifteen then, perhaps because my own physical maturity came rather late or perhaps because I was just absentminded, I did not clearly comprehend that Onēsama had been the cause of my parents' divorce. But I did know enough to keep the fact that I often dropped into Onēsama's ikebana classes on the way home from school a secret from my mother. There I would listen to the pleasing rhythmical click of her shears, the sound of which reminded me of nursery men, as her big, beautiful hands encased in work gloves cut through the thick flower branches that her students lacked the physical strength or muscle to cut themselves. Beads of perspiration bathed the glossy nape of her neck, as smooth as if freshly shaven, over which fell a few loose strands of hair. Much to the amusement of the women of various ages who attended her classes, I would press my best lace handkerchief—that I had carefully made more absorbent by soaking in water before ironing to remove the excess starch—against the perspiration on the nape of her neck. "Why don't you do ikebana?" one of the women asked. "But Haruna doesn't need other flowers when she has our teacher," another observed, laughing.

When this happened, Onēsama would smile, remove her work gloves, and thank me. However, she also added, "You see, Haruna, I wear the gloves of a physical laborer so perhaps I should wear a towel around my neck like a worker rather than your pretty lace handkerchief. Don't you think so? Look at the muscles in my right arm."

Some time later when my mother was out of the house one day, my brother said, "That woman's no good. She's bad. So don't ever go back to those ikebana classes again. You're sixteen, aren't you? How can you be so stupid? Are you backward or something?" Then he sniggered, "Don't you know that your Onēsama is Dad's lover?"

"You're lying," I cried. "That can't be right."

"It's true," my brother said, "and you're the only person who doesn't know it."

"No! It's a lie," I cried once more.

"Why won't you believe it?" he said. "You're old enough to face reality. Or did she tell you not to believe any rumors you might hear?"

"She never said anything like that," I defended Onēsama. "That's a terrible lie."

"What an idiot you are," retorted my brother.

"But Onēsama is 173 centimeters tall. Dad's so short. He's hardly even 160 centimeters," I argued.

"Moron! Is that what you really think?" my brother said. "Dad might be short but he's got plenty of money."

I felt my bosom tighten and, gasping for breath, dashed to my room where, in a fit of tears, I locked myself in. A feeling of emptiness swept over me as if I was seriously ill. I did not have the courage to confirm my brother's claims and so I just stopped seeing Onēsama. But before long, I read in a weekly magazine that my father and Onēsama had been married. Once I knew that, I did my best to forget all about her. And as for our shawls with the embroidered rambling roses, I was so distressed that I took my light pink wrap, which complemented her rose pink one, and shredded it to pieces with my sewing scissors. Not only did my fingers and arm ache from the effort, but I was also left with a lingering awareness of my own pettiness.

That was twenty-five years ago when Onēsama was twenty-nine. A friend and I recently went back to the site of the old home. "If you still owned this, it'd be worth at least three billion yen," he said like a real estate agent. I stood, lost in thought, wondering what had happened to the weeping cherry, the willows and the sasanqua camellias.

Just then, a white limousine taxi pulled up outside the building. A tall woman with grey hair got out and made her way up the tiled stairs of the hall. She was wearing a *hakata* obi around her subdued *ōshima* fabric kimono. The air was dry and it was doubtless the static electricity that made her hem rise and fall four or five centimeters with each step she took, momentarily revealing the kimono's light blue lining. Halfway up the stairs, she stopped and turned briefly. I saw that the cord securing her obi was the same color as her kimono lining. As she began once again to climb the stairs, I caught a seductive glimpse of the red silk that lined her kimono sleeves. Certainly, this had to be Onēsama. Suddenly, the chauffeur of the limousine taxi ran up the stairs after her. "You forgot this, Madam" he said, handing her something. It was the rose pink shawl with the unmistakably characteristic cutwork along both edges. "My," I thought, "how thrifty of her still to have that shawl after all this time." ♋

* * *

"Well, I'll be traveling around Italy for a month or two," said my aunt, which didn't necessarily make me all that envious, but, since I felt a bit bad that I didn't feel more envious, I said "Lucky you. Italy will certainly be warmer." She looked at me. "You're not too good at geography, are you?" she said. "Except for the Naples region, the northern part of Italy near the Alps is extremely cold." This reminded me of the story of Hannibal whose legions were able to cross the snow-covered Alps by elephant and conduct a surprise invasion of the Roman Empire. "But," I replied, "even African elephants made it over the Alps so, it might be cold, but it's not the North Pole, you know." My aunt looked worried. "I'm not sure that someone who says such odd things is capable of looking after herself—even for a month or two," she said. Then she added, "Do you think you'll be lonely by yourself?"

"You must be joking," I said. "Heaps of my friends from university live alone."

"I'm sure they do. Sorry. Sorry. For a moment there I sounded like a mother," said my aunt, laughing and poking out her tongue. "I don't think there'll be too much to worry about but since we are in an old building you never know when there'll be a problem with the plumbing or the hot water system or the heating—but I'm sure you'll be able to manage if that happens." She was due to depart in a week and there were all sorts of things that had to be arranged.

Even though it certainly wasn't the first time my aunt had ever gone overseas she seemed to be quite elated about the prospect of traveling, and I was so swept up in her mood that I felt quite excited myself. We both saw red, however, when my mother made her usual phone call the Sunday evening before my aunt left and started going on in a panic when she found out that Auntie was going away. "You're so irresponsible," my mother accused my aunt. "There I was, trusting Momoko to your care. That makes you her guardian while she's in Tokyo. Maybe if you were only going for a couple of weeks, I wouldn't mind so much. But one or two months overseas? I'm very upset about this."

"Stop carrying on," my aunt replied. "She's twenty. Of course she can manage on her own for a month or two."

"Well, that may be," replied my mother. "But, unlike you, I never had a chance to live away from home without my parents. And I've had to carry on the family business all by myself. It's alright for you to say I'm taking things too seriously but I've never had the same freedom as you." This was what my mother seemed to be saying at the other end of the phone as a full-scale argument erupted between the pair.

I took the phone in the middle of their altercation. "Just because you're on your own, don't think you can go doing anything bad," my mother nagged. "What do you mean, 'anything bad'?" I asked her. "You know," she said, "anything bad. Of course you know what I mean. I mean anything bad," she said repeating the same words over and over as she always did. "Look," I said. "I'm not in kindergarten you know. I'll be fine by myself. I wanted to live by myself in Tokyo anyway." She sniffed and ignored me. "Well," she said, "make sure you turn the gas off before you go out. When you came home for the summer vacation, you were smoking, weren't you? If you go smoking in bed you'll start a fire. And don't let the dirty washing pile up. By the way, tell your aunt to make sure she gives me a call before she leaves for Italy." With that final demand, my mother hung up.

When I got off the phone, it didn't take long for an argument to develop also between my aunt and me. "You should never have said anything to that sister of mine about the trip," my aunt said. "Then you should have told me not to say anything," I countered. "She just asked how you were and all I said was,

'She's fine, she's getting ready to go on a trip.' And then she asked where you were going, so I told her. 'Italy.' That's all I said," I defended myself. "Well, you said too much. The last thing I needed was to have to listen to her droning on endlessly about nothing."

Hanako and I went off to Narita to say goodbye to my aunt, who was having difficulty managing the bulky insulated raincoat made out of slippery nylon twill that she was carrying. "So, do you think I should give you a little reward for coming to see me off? Or would you prefer a present from Italy?" she asked us.

"A present, a present," cried Hanako.

"Both, both," I replied.

"Okay then, you can eat pizza and drink Chianti at Shark in Mejiro," she said, handing over 20,000 yen as she disappeared with a wave of her hand down the stairs to the Alitalia ticket gate. "Bye-bye," we called, waving. "See you when I get back," cried my aunt, with a smile. "I'll look after Momoko," Hanako called.

"Your aunt is going to eat real Italian food and all we get to do is eat pizza in Mejiro. Oh well, bad luck," said Hanako, eating a pizza piled with cheese and slivers of garlic. "You know, it might only be a month, but I really envy you living on your own. Even when I graduate and start earning money, there'll be a huge outburst from Dad if I so much as think about leaving home."

"Will there?" I asked. Then I added, "Hey, Hanako, why don't you stay at my place tonight?"

"Really? Are you lonely already?"

"Of course not. That's not why I'm asking."

"I wouldn't mind staying."

"Will it be okay with your Dad?"

"Yeah, but he'll say something sarcastic afterwards, like,

'You're not a stray cat. You shouldn't go round staying at people's places.'"

"I think he mistakes you for a girl from a good family."

"Maybe he does. He's such a pain."

We drank a bottle of Chianti as we ate our way through the garlic pizza, an anchovy pizza, Milanese-style veal cutlets, lasagna and a green salad, by which time we were full and only had change of 3,600 yen from our first 10,000. It was a bit extravagant. "But, never mind," I thought to myself. "We did use the reward money that Auntie gave us." On our way home we stopped at the Tanakaya liquor store in front of the station to buy a bottle of Beaujolais Nouveau—I remembered my aunt had previously told me that the only drinkable Beaujolais was Nouveau—and knowing that we had bought a palatable wine put Hanako and me in very high spirits.

"Let's put a table out on the verandah for lunch tomorrow," Hanako suggested. "We can look at the autumn leaves in the garden of Gakushūin while we eat *croque monsieur* and drink Beaujolais." "Sounds good," I thought to myself, "except those idiot cheer squads from Gakushūin might be screaming and chanting up on the school roof and the sound is sure to travel over to us." But I said nothing and just agreed.

After ten days or so a postcard with a picture of Fra Angelico arrived from Florence. "It's colder here than I'd expected," wrote my aunt, "but I've still been doing the rounds of the art galleries and cathedrals. For the past twenty years or so, there's been a serial killer who goes around the town on moonless nights shooting couples on lovers' trysts. There were two shootings recently, one after the other. So once night falls, young couples are nowhere to be seen. But since we're not young, it's quite safe for us to go out at night walking." I noticed that she said "we," which certainly explained a few things.

Hanako received a second card saying that my aunt had

traveled from Florence to San Gimignano, a medieval fortress town, and that she had frostbite on her little toe from walking on freezing cold flagstones there.

As usual, I spent my time doing pretty well nothing and skipped most lectures just to lie around sleeping instead. In fact, I was astounded at my own capacity for sleep because although I wasn't unwell—nor do I tire all that easily—I found I had no trouble sleeping deeply for sixteen hours at a stretch. Now and again I would wake up momentarily, go to the toilet, and then stretch to loosen my body after being curled up for so long, but then I'd just crawl back into bed and go straight back to sleep.

If the phone rang I assumed that it would be to do with my aunt's work and that I'd be no help except to tell the caller that Auntie was away on a trip so I just pulled the blanket up over my head, let the phone ring, and then went back to sleep. After a week of this it became difficult to tell the difference between reality and all the dreams I was having because, even though I'd been asleep for most of the time, it seemed as if I'd been quite active and done all sorts of things. But enough of my dreams, that's a completely different story.

Eventually, a phone call came from Hanako. "You haven't been at school for ages," she said, "and every time I ring there's no answer. What's going on?"

"Well," I replied. "I've been really busy."

"What?? Busy? That's pretty unusual isn't it," teased Hanako, sounding amazed. "What on earth have you been doing?" she asked in a puzzled voice.

"Nothing in particular," I told her. "I've just been busy sleeping everyday."

"I think I know what you mean," said Hanako. "You know those fellows who quote Paul Nizan," she continued. "He said, 'I was twenty years old. I will let no one say that this is the best time of life.' A student from Tokyo University who used to come to the house as my tutor told me that."

"Yeah," I said, "I've heard it too. But does anyone really ever say that being twenty is the best time of life? Or am I wrong, maybe? Is being young actually supposed to be so wonderful?"

"That's precisely what I'm trying to say. Don't you think that being twenty is the very time you want to sleep the most?"

Hanako, who was actually as good at sleeping as I was, would have spent every day asleep if she'd had the chance and had no difficulty sleeping ten hours at a stretch. Her mother nagged her constantly about this, much to Hanako's annoyance.

While sleeping, I dreamt that I was riding on all sort of vehicles—trains, cars, boats, Ferris-wheels and bikes—and I also seemed to be walking around the streets of a city, although sometimes I made and ate meals and I even watched movies and read books. "But," I said to Hanako as I scrawled something, as a child might, in the layer of fluffy white dust on the top of the bookshelf, "I wonder if I really should spend my time sleeping like this—it's pretty complacent." Hanako's reply was rather trite. "It's people who are suppressed," she said, "who have dreams, you know." I suddenly found her rather irritating. She'd rung to see if she could come over as her Dad was away for the night because of the funeral of a writer who lived somewhere outside Tokyo. "Sure," I said. "Come on round." But I actually thought it would be a bit of a bother and would really rather have been on my own.

Since in the ten days or so in question I clearly hadn't felt like doing anything but sleeping, I'd spent the whole time in the tracksuit I used as pajamas, and, although this outfit was off-white to start with, it had now turned a dingy sort of grey, a bit like a cat that'd been rolling around in the dirt under a verandah. I'd just pulled on a raincoat over the top to go to the supermarket, had eaten nothing but frozen Chinese buns, had only bathed once and hadn't bothered to wash my face. Neither had I tidied my room. The television was broken—but I didn't feel like watching anything, anyway—and since I didn't even want to listen to music, I did absolutely nothing at all except sleep.

At one point a call came from my mother. "Are you doing the right thing?" she asked. "Yes, I'm doing the right thing," I answered as, ignoring the torrent of words that followed, I pulled the collar of my tracksuit top round to my nose and smelt it instead—while it stank of sour sweat and certainly wasn't too fragrant, I was all the same quite impressed by the fact that my body could make such a smell.

I hadn't had a bath or changed my tracksuit since my mother's phone call so I decided to have a shower before Hanako arrived. I felt quite chilled coming out of the shower and, even though the heater was on, was a bit worried I might catch a cold.

Hanako arrived after racing over on her bike, pajamas and toiletries in her backpack. She obviously thought that she looked very cool in black bike pants, black bulky sweater, and red basketball shoes, and she was pretty shocked to see the room littered with newspapers, magazines, teacups and the leftovers of frozen meat buns. "Are you okay?" she asked. "Have you been sick?" She looked around the room in amazement.

Sick? "Maybe," I thought. "I have had a touch of depression." My hair was still wet after being washed and, since it was making my ear itchy, I scratched at this with a cotton bud while Hanako started tidying up. "I've just remembered," she said. "I've got a present for you. There's an old-style candy store near my house and they had this lying around in the dust. It's pretty good value for a 130 yen, don't you think?"

She ceremoniously took a brown paper bag out of her backpack. "Close your eyes," she said cheerily and, when I did, I felt two hands stretch out followed by the sensation of thick cold plastic against both sides of my face as she put a pair of glasses on me. "Go on," said Hanako. "Open your eyes." Perhaps she expected me to say that her face and everything around her shone with a rose-colored glow, but it wasn't really like that—it was more like I was looking at things through a pale red lens.

"You see," said Hanako, "when you put these on, it's 'Rose C'est la Vie.' Pretty sexy, aren't they?" I realized she probably meant to say "La Vie en Rose" so I laughed and replied, "The world certainly does look rosy."

"That's not all," Hanako said loudly. She brought a hand mirror from the bathroom cupboard and held it up in front of my face.

In the mirror I saw tousled half-wet hair above a pair of toy-like sunglasses with pink heart-shaped frames and red lenses that gave a glow to the smiling face of a young woman—although on closer inspection you could see that her skin was rough and her lips were peeling from neglect. Still, the girl—who, of course, was me—did have a smile on her face, so she didn't look too unhappy. "They're Lolita sunglasses," said Hanako. "Have you ever seen them before?"

"Yes," I replied. "I saw them in the movie a few years ago. Where I grew up they had a show called *Afternoon Hollywood Classics* on a local channel and I used to go home early from school if there was something I wanted to see."

"Wow, you lucky thing," said Hanako. "I've only seen stills. *Lolita*'s a Stanley Kubrick movie, isn't it?"

"That's right," I answered. "I read Nabokov's novel a while after I saw the movie and was surprised because it didn't seem like the sort of thing that Kubrick would make into a film— Lolita was played by a girl actor or maybe a teenager called Sue Lyon who was pretty fat and who had a wicked-looking, unpleasant sort of face. Why don't you try the glasses on?" I said to Hanako.

"Unfortunately, I can't," Hanako said. "It's impossible. I'm so short-sighted that without my own glasses I can't even see the lines on the palm of my hand if it's more than ten centimeters from my face. I once tried contacts, but I washed two pairs down the hand-basin sink. After the second time, my parents refused to replace them."

"Have a go at putting them on anyway," I said. I took the heart-shaped glasses off and handed them to her. Hanako took off her own glasses. In old Hollywood films or comics for teenage girls, women often remove their glasses and then let down long hair which up until that point has usually been drawn back fiercely. This is the sign of a complete change in their personalities as they suddenly astound everyone in the movie and in the audience by becoming ravishing beauties bathed in soft light. But, since all that is fantasy, when Hanako took off her glasses she merely looked more childish—and since she had no hair to let down, removing the glasses only made her look more and more like a boy. I must have smiled as all this was going through my head because Hanako seemed to know what I was thinking and snorted with exasperation in a more exaggerated manner than usual. "The image of a woman removing her glasses," she declared, "has been constructed to represent the self-protective virginal woman with her newly found modern subjectivity letting down her defenses. This," she continued, "is because spectacles are equated with intelligence." With that, she put on the heart-shaped glasses. "What do you think?" she asked. "Do they suit me?" She stood posing with her chin in the air.

"They do suit you. You look good," I said. "You look really cute." I looked at her and giggled. "What is it? Do I look sexy?" she asked again. I handed her the mirror which she held ten centimeters away from her face as she peered closely at herself. "I look like a rabbit on heat," she said, doing a couple of bunny-hops. We burst out laughing together.

With that, I changed out of my pajamas for the first time in a while and, after deciding to walk to Takadanobaba to buy something to eat for dinner, we crossed the Kanda River, took some back streets and came out at the Pearl Cinema where we bumped into my aunt's photographer friend, Natsuyuki. "Hi there, Momoko," he said, "Long time no see." So I said, "Do you feel like taking us somewhere for a cup of tea?" "Okay," he said. "But just tea." We crossed the road and went into a coffee shop.

111

❦

We went with Natsuyuki to a coffee shop and bar done in a sort of American colonial–style, one of those places where they have personalized bourbon bottles lined up for the regular customers—a case of Takadanobaba doing its best to be Shibuya. Now Hanako might be short, but she's got a really loud voice and she doesn't know the meaning of the word "restraint," so as we walked in, she yelled out, "Look at this place, will you. Here we are in Takadanobaba but they've decked the place out like it's in Shibuya. What wankers." Everyone stared, with the waiters and bartenders glaring at us with particular outrage.

It had rightly occurred to me that Natsuyuki wouldn't have anything terribly enlightening to say. "I've got no work," he began. Then he continued. "I've just seen *Paris Texas* and it's really boring. Wim Wenders is a terrible director."

Hanako had never met Natsuyuki before and she was pretty taken aback at what he had to say about Wenders. "That's crap," she protested in her roughest boy talk. "He's great." This time it was Natsuyuki who looked shocked since he clearly hadn't heard too many girls or young women speak like Hanako and, although it occurred to me that I hadn't actually introduced the pair, it wasn't really necessary because as soon as I said the name of one, the other said, "Oh, so you're ..." After that, the conversation became more lively and eventually it was somehow decided that at five o'clock we'd meet a friend of Natsuyuki's, an accountant who lived in Tokorozawa, at the Big Box coffee shop in Takadanobaba. Then I got carried away and asked everyone over to my aunt's place in Mejiro for dinner, after which I was immediately gripped by an attack of "mother" disease and wondered whether this would be okay while my aunt was away.

Hanako looked at me and realized this. "Her aunt asked me to come over and stay with her while she was by herself," she said to Natsuyuki and his friend, "but I don't know what she would think about a couple of middle-aged men like you two." Natsuyuki and his friend looked at each other and laughed.

"Don't be so silly, darling. I've known your aunt since before you two were born," said the accountant friend. His voice was rather camp, but he had a crew-cut, a masculine, suntanned face and wore a navy blue French zip-up jacket over a white T-shirt and white BD undershirt with blue jeans and sneakers that were washed lily white. Everything about him was clean-looking, a bit too clean, in fact. "And I even know your dear mother," he said to me. "I met her at Chieko's apartment. That pair certainly have different personalities. Do you take after your Mama?"

"I don't think so," I replied.

"She's more like her aunt," said Natsuyuki. "She sleeps for ten hours a day. Anyway, what are we going to eat?" he asked. "I think we were having beef stew," Hanako answered. But the accountant said, "Are you going shopping now to make stew? Won't it take too long to prepare? Of course I don't know what sort of stew you had in mind," he said, sounding like a connoisseur. "Okay then," said Natsuyuki to his friend. "Why don't you make us something?" And we said, "Yes, please, Ken. We'd love you to make dinner."

Although Ken was fairly old, since Natsuyuki introduced him by merely saying, "This is Ken-chan. He's an accountant," we had no option but just to call him Ken. We arrived at the Peacock Supermarket right when it was most crowded and, although it seemed pretty unnecessary for all of us to go in, since I had nothing for breakfast next morning and since I also needed to buy a few essentials like toilet paper and washing powder, the four of us all eventually filed into the crowded store. "I'll get the things we need for tonight," said Ken. Making his way around the shelves in the food section, he looked as if he knew exactly what he was doing and, thinking that he was perhaps a chef and not an accountant, I wondered if I'd heard correctly when Natsuyuki did the introductions. Hanako was over at the cosmetics counter where there were hardly any customers and where she was in the middle of painting each of her fingernails with nail polish from red, yellow and green testers. "What are you doing?" I asked. "There's no nail polish remover at home. You'd better get that stuff off before you leave." I could hear myself sounding just like my mother again. "Natsuyuki said that guy's an accountant, didn't he?" I checked with Hanako. "He's not a chef, is he?" Hanako hummed a tune. "Well, he will be the chef tonight," was all she had to say. "Mm, that's true," I thought and then decided to try some mascara with a special eyelash lengthening fiber.

"Hey, you'd better not do that," said Hanako, as I went to pick up the mascara tester. "Why not?" I asked.

"You'll get a chalazion," she said.

"What's that?" I said.

"A sty," she explained. "How do you know that someone with a sty hasn't used that tester?" Hanako looked serious as she added, "They're not hygienic, you know, these sorts of cosmetic testers."

Just then, along came Natsuyuki and Ken, their shopping baskets piled with groceries. They apparently overheard us. "Yes, you should be careful," said Ken. "I once heard a story about gonorrhea being spread through a whole sewing school because in the olden days the girls at those schools shared the water pipe they used to blow water to dampen the clothes when ironing."

"Are you sure that really happened?" asked Natsuyuki dubiously.

"It certainly did. It was all because nutrition was so bad in those days. Of course no one uses that sort of water pipe when they're ironing these days. But in those days," Ken explained, "lots of girls had mouth ulcers. All those complaints are transmitted through mucous membranes. Even in public baths, girls could catch trichomonas and end up with a terrible vaginal discharge. So they used to tell young women not to sit directly on the tiles at the public bath. In the past they gave that sort of advice in the medical pages of magazines for young people."

"What's that? What's a trichomona?" Hanako called out at the top of her voice.

"Don't be so dreadful," said Ken, blushing with embarrassment, even though he had started the conversation. "You shouldn't call out like that."

The menu was headed with endive halves topped with a walnut dressing over sliced onion, sautéed as it might have been for onion gratin. "Ken actually brought the dressing with him from home," said Natsuyuki. "He brought it back for me from France as a present. Apparently he tasted some in a restaurant in Paris and thought it was absolutely delicious." The endive was followed by marinated mushrooms, while the main dish was a paella with calamari, prawns, cod, clams and smaller shell fish, all cooked in a big earthenware pot. "We need some greens with this, don't we?" said Ken. He brought out a salad of fresh spring chrysanthemum leaves topped with crunchy fried bacon bits. We washed the meal down with glasses of sangria. Ken-chan was an excellent cook and, not only was he quick and efficient, he was also very neat and tidied everything up carefully so that Natsuyuki, Hanako and myself did absolutely nothing. Ken, who was showing no sign of tiring, then suggested that we go to a gay bar. "Fine," said Natsuyuki. "But on the way I want to drop by the house and give the cat something to eat." So we ladled the leftover paella into a tupperware container to give to the cat and set out on the seven- or eight-minute walk to Natsuyuki's apartment. "My Tama isn't used to the smell of saffron," said Natsuyuki, "so I'm not sure if she's going to eat this." Ken told Natsuyuki not to worry. "The rain in Spain stays mainly in the plain" said Ken, "and the cats in Spain eat mainly leftover paella."

After our night out I realized that the mild depression I'd suffered for a while seemed to have disappeared, and while I wouldn't have gone so far as to say that things were looking rosy, I definitely didn't feel too bad, so I went back to university and went out occasionally and enjoyed myself, eventually going back home at the end of December to see in the New Year with my mother, my younger brother and my grandmother. My mother was really hyped up about the fact that my brother would soon sit for his entrance exams, while it seemed to me that my brother had no hope of passing. "What's the point in trying to be a doctor?" I asked him. "Why don't you forget about that and just take over the family business?" Although my mother was furious when I said this and we had quite an argument, Jun'ichi himself said vaguely, "You might be right. It'd be depressing to be a doctor, anyway." "Yes," I said, "they're both service industries and you'd be better off running the inn." As I said this it occurred to me that perhaps this brother with whom I didn't get on very well might have had a different father, something that certainly wasn't impossible.

On the evening of January sixth a telephone call came from Hanako who told me something that, in one way, gave us a reason to celebrate New Year. "My parents haven't been getting along all that well since last year but, anyway, they've decided to get a divorce. I'll never understand either of them but they're both saying that this might be a good chance for me to set up by myself. They're so selfish." That, pretty well, was what she told me on the phone, at which point I had a brilliant idea. "Well, then," I said, "why don't we rent a flat together?" Hanako laughed. "That's really why I rang," she explained. "Luckily the apartment next to Natsuyuki's will be vacant from February. My mother and father were both pretty impressed with how well-mannered and refined the landlady was and so it was all arranged today."

"Wow, that was quick."

"It sure was," answered Hanako. "I'll tell you all about how it happened when I see you. It's got two little bedrooms, a kitchen and a bathroom. The rent's 70,000 yen per month and it's pretty old and dirty."

In spite of the fact that the apartment we intended to rent was only seven or eight minutes walk to my aunt's and that when you divided the rent in half it was only 35,000 yen a month, my mother wasn't very happy. However, Hanako spoke to her on the phone very politely and graciously. "I don't wish to be immodest," Hanako said gravely to my mother, "but I'm very responsible. Since I was small I've kept a strict record of my pocket money expenses. And I'm not just a friend of Momoko's, I'm extremely lucky to know her aunt in Mejiro, too. The apartment's called the Red Plum Lodge. It's very nice and quiet. Would you mind holding on for a minute. I'll put you on to my father." She very adeptly smoothed my mother's ruffled feathers.

"Well," said my mother finally, "I think you should at least wait until your aunt returns from Italy before you move house. Don't you think it's a bit rude to leave while she's away?" she persisted. "Mom," I said, exasperated, "you're so slow. You just don't get it, do you? My aunt decided to go to Italy because she was sick of having me there." It was pretty thoughtless of me to have said this and, as soon as the words came out, I realized that I'd made a huge strategic blunder because, somehow, it gave my mother reason to turn her anger on me. "Your Aunt Chieko is your own flesh and blood," she said. "Since you were small she's been fonder of you than Jun'ichi. But you've obviously taken advantage of that. You know what sort of work she does. You should have been more considerate of her. I heard what you said yesterday to poor Jun'ichi even though he's a bundle of nerves. I've never met anyone so cruel and heartless." By now, I was pretty annoyed too, but realizing that withdrawal would be the better course of action, I merely said, "I think it would be best if

I moved house as soon as possible," and went off into my room. While I was sipping the expensive cognac I'd stolen from the living room and hidden away, there was a knock at the door and Jun'ichi came in with two glasses and the bottle of Suntory Old Whiskey that he'd also probably stolen earlier. He gave a sideways glance at the cognac I was drinking. "Look at that," he said with a sigh. "Even when I steal booze, I'm pretty timid. You know, I did pretty badly in the trial exam we had the other day. I'd really like to leave home as soon as possible, like you have. And I think I'll have some of that too," he said, pouring himself a glass of cognac. "By the way, I've decided to go into the family business," he told me, and then he asked, "What are you going to do when you graduate?" Thinking that this brother of mine wasn't so bad after all, I said "That's good," in response to his first statement, and then, "I have no idea," in reply to his question.

I went back to Mejiro on the tenth. It was quite difficult to open the door to my aunt's apartment as there was a big mountain of magazines and post-cards piled up behind the letterbox in the dust-covered entrance to the apartment. As I tidied these up, I found a postcard from my aunt saying that she would be home at the end of the month. There was still quite a lot I had to do so I decided to move house some time in February. Hanako's mother had already moved out to Hanako's grandmother's house. "There's no way I can bear to live together in a house with that old man of mine," said Hanako. "He's fat, he's so old-fashioned and he's totally self-centered. He studied theatre, you see, and my Mom was in the same class as him. It's just too depressing to have to live with that sort of sex-crazed man. Just the thought of it fills me with despair." So, after packing everything and sending it by delivery service to my aunt's place, Hanako came over on her bicycle.

"He tried to seduce a woman in such a cheap and miserable way," Hanako told me. "I feel so embarrassed. Your Dad wouldn't do anything like that."

"I don't know whether he would or not," I said. "Besides, you know his boyfriend problems."

"Still," pondered Hanako, "he's not into sexual harassment, is he?"

"I'm not really sure," I replied. "The way he employs the bell-boys at the hotel is a bit suspicious."

I watched as Hanako took a stuffed Steiff crow with red legs and beak out of a cardboard box.

"Hey, I've got one of those too," I told her. "My Dad bought it for me when I was little. I left it at my mother's place. I should have brought it with me."

"Mine came from my Mom's brother when I was in primary school," she said. "He used to live in France." With that she plonked down on the floor and said, "Oh, I'm so tired. But I'm glad it's all over."

By now, night had fallen, so we decided to wait till the following day to go and look at our rooms at the Red Plum Lodge. For dinner we ate steamed rice, some sea urchin I'd brought from home, seaweed flakes and pickled vegetables, toasting ourselves with a little leftover sake to celebrate the start of our new lives.

When we went to Red Plum Lodge the following day we were greeted by a black and white cat sitting in the window of Natsuyuki's apartment. It meowed as it saw us. "Looks like we'll be good friends with this cat," we said to each other as we went into the apartment with the key the elderly landlady gave us.

"This is not bad at all," I thought. There was a spacious garden with a plum tree and one of the two windows facing the garden opened out onto a verandah. I really liked the fact that you could go straight from the house onto the verandah and had the decadent feeling that I'd be spending all my time just lying out there in the sun. Natsuyuki came in, having heard the sound of our chatting and the windows opening. "O-oh," he said. "So you two are my new neighbors."

"Yes," we said. "We hope you won't mind if we call on you for help every now and then."

Then Hanako asked, "What's the cat's name?"

"Tama," said Natsuyuki. "But it's not my cat."

The cat jumped down off the window ledge and strode across the garden where it leapt up onto a stone lantern. From there it jumped up into the plum tree and, curling up its legs, settled down into a fork between two branches.

"How about a cup of tea?" asked Natsuyuki. "Yes, please," we both answered. "Well, then," he said, "come on in." We went into his apartment from the verandah and began chatting.

"When's Chieko coming home?" he asked.

"She said in a postcard around the end of the month," I told him.

"I see."

"Yeah, that's what she said."

"Is that a male cat?" asked Hanako.

"No, it's a girl," said Natsuyuki. "She had kittens just the other day."

"She's really big, isn't she?"

"She was pretty big for a female cat," explained Natsuyuki, "even before she had the kittens."

"But she's really nice, though," said Hanako. "I didn't mean that there was anything wrong with her. I like that kind of cat."

"But why did you call her a boring old name like Tama?" I asked.

"I'm not the person who named her," said Natsuyuki.

After chatting for a while, Hanako and I had a bit of an argument about who would use which room. Neither of us had any desire to decorate our rooms in a girly fashion. "I might not bother with a bed and just use a futon," I said. "You can use more of the room that way. There are two large single closets so there'll be no problems putting our things away. What do you think we should do about furniture for the kitchen? We certainly need to buy a set of table and chairs so we'll have to go and look for some before too long. It would be good if my father could buy us a set as a house-warming present. And we've got to buy curtains. Of course, we could just bring the ones from our old rooms. But this is the start of our new life so we should try and at least get ourselves new curtains."

As we spoke we became quite animated and realized that there would be a long list of things we needed to buy.

"Okay, okay," said Natsuyuki, "you might need a list, but do you think you could make that up when you go home?" He was clearly a bit fed up with our chatting. "Sorry, sorry," we said. "We'll bring you some house-warming noodles later." He thanked us rather flatly. "What's wrong?" we asked. "None of your business," he replied.

Well, everyone gets a bit down in dumps now and again and it was true that it was none of our business. So we said, "Okay, we'll see you soon," and then rode our bikes back to my aunt's apartment where we made up our list eating doughnuts.

When the list was complete I wondered vaguely how our new life would turn out. Hanako was singing a Southern All Stars song while she looked at some magazines. "Perhaps I should become a photographer," she said. "They seem to have a lot of spare time."

"Perhaps," I said, "but then a novelist probably has more."

"You might be right," said Hanako. "There must be some job that will still pay the bills but let me do what I like."

This was something I'd also been thinking about.

"Yeah," I agreed, "there must be something." I'd wanted to read Flaubert's *Sentimental Education* for a while, so I took it down from my aunt's bookshelf and began reading.

12

∾

I lay on the verandah and looked at the garden as Tama, the cat, played with one of her kittens. Of course, it was the kitten that was actually doing the playing. Tama, the mother, was really only trying to catch the kitten with her paws, push it down and lick its fur.

The elderly landlady brought a saucer of milk. "Tama," she called, "would you like something to drink?" I sat up and said hello. "I wonder," said the landlady, "why mother cats get so carried away grooming their kittens? It's not so bad if the kittens are this size, but I've read in Konrad Lorenz's book on animal behavior that when a mother cat cleans her newborn she can use so much force that she ends up eating the kitten." "Oh, is that so?" I said. Just then, I saw my aunt wave her hand from behind the hedge fence. "Hi," I called. Since my aunt and the elderly landlady knew each other quite well, the landlady offered my aunt some tea. So Hanako, my aunt, Natsuyuki, the elderly landlady and I all drank tea together on the verandah.

"There're lots of houses being torn down," said my aunt, "even in a quiet area like this." "Well," said the landlady, "since they decided to shift the metropolitan office to Shinjuku, land values in the area have soared. We have real estate agents and condominium agents coming all the time to try and get us to exchange this house and land for an apartment of equal value. My son and daughter are worried about the inheritance tax and say it's better to try and do something while their father is still alive. But it's all very difficult. I'm in good health, and although my husband has a touch of dementia, physically he's still quite okay and would like to stay here. So we've no intention of selling."

We all breathed a sigh of relief to hear her say this. After the landlady left, Natsuyuki told us a story about her husband's dementia. "I met him in the garden once and he mistook me for his grandson," said Natsuyuki. "He made me take 1,000 yen note."

"I wonder if he's got any granddaughters," said Hanako.

"I don't think so," said Natsuyuki. "But don't worry, Hanako," he added, laughing, "you could easily get your thousand yen by being mistaken for his schoolboy grandson." Several days later that's exactly what happened.

Natsuyuki's cat was apparently forced onto him by someone who demanded that he look after her whether he wanted to or not. This cat had had five kittens, four of which had been given away. The fifth one went to the elderly landlady.

In spite of the fact that I was starting a new life in a new home, I didn't feel all that refreshed. Even when Hanako invited me to go with her to a movie or to a show at the theatre, I usually said, "Why don't you go by yourself?" Most days, I just lay around as before, not doing very much at all.

The narrator of Evelyn Waugh's novel, *Brideshead Revisited*, goes to stay at the baroque sixteenth century castle of one of his Oxford classmates where the pair spends their time lying around just drinking wine from the castle cellar, starting with a fine white at midday, and engaging in melancholy and sensual conversation.

"I wonder if we should be doing this?" says one.

"Of course we should," says the other.

Even though, in my case, the sensual element was lacking, I often played both roles.

"I wonder if I should be doing this," I'd ask myself.

"Of course you should," I'd reply.

"There's nothing wrong with that," said my aunt, laughing, when I told her about this. "That scene, by the way, is the most decadent in the whole novel. Anyway, you shouldn't worry about anything. When the time comes for you to do something, you'll do it, even if you don't want to. So meanwhile," she said in a leisurely tone, "just read a book or do whatever you like. There's no need to worry about things until the time comes to do them." Then she recalled, "You know, when I was your age I was already writing novels. And, how can I put it, I was also more interested in things, including sex. I had so many boyfriends I could get rid of the ones I wasn't interested in without a second thought. Certainly I was more energetic than I am now. But these days I play both parts in *Passing of the Day* by Shimao Toshio. When Shimao had writer's block, his wife, Miho, would tell him, 'Dear, even one page will bring in some money.' But I have to say this to myself. And that's the truth."

"You're right," said Natsuyuki, "everything is such a bother. I've got a friend who always says he wishes he could spend his whole life being a bit tipsy. Yoshida Ken'ichi and Uchida Hyakken probably thought the same thing as well."

"I'd say both those men were more drunk than just tipsy," said my aunt. And so the conversation took a decidedly middle-aged turn. What with the elderly landlady and landlord and Natsuyuki as my neighbors, my surroundings seemed to become sort of desexed after I moved into Red Plum Lodge. Even though at university there were lots of girls with long straight hair who laughed as they breathed in, instead of out, sounding as if they were having an orgasm, and even though Hanako's Dad had his young lover while mine seemed to have a young male lover, it was too much of a bother for me to go out with boys, whose conversation, anyway, bored me to tears.

Hanako said that, once exams finished, she would spend time during the spring vacation working in the pie and terrine shop that was formerly owned by her aunt but which, since her parents' divorce, had been jointly run by her mother and her mother's elder sister. Although I didn't really intend to, it just so happened that I also found work in the kitchen of this little shop in a residential area of Ogikubo, where day after day—it was really only for ten days—I stirred gelatinous mince with a moulinette and stuffed little pie shells with white sauce and crab. Since Hanako's mother's friends and acquaintances placed lots of special orders to celebrate the start of her new life and her new business, both Hanako and I stirred the moulinette round and round for all we were worth in order to make dozens of authentic home-cooked terrines which we baked in a mould and then stored for ten days in the refrigerator. "I think," Hanako announced energetically, "that I'll take one of these as a sample to your Dad's hotel and get orders for the restaurant." Her enthusiasm was catching and, thinking about the wild boar hotpot and venison sashimi that were winter specialties at my mother's inn, I suggested to Hanako's mother that she make a terrine from wild boar or venison. "Mmm, what a good idea," she replied enthusiastically. "It's very important to develop new products." Although we were soon pretty bored, when I received my pay of 35,000 yen for working five hours a day for ten days—which, by the way, was my first pay ever—I felt quite happy and thought I would get work again in the summer holidays.

I'm still not totally satisfied with the way things are, but neither do I have any special need to search for my real self or to do anything in particular. So for the time being, I'll just continue like this.

On the last day of our part-time job, Hanako's mother and aunt took Hanako and me for a meal at Kokeshiya French restaurant. "Women need to make themselves independent," said Hanako's mother. "Your mother, for example, Momoko, runs an inn all by herself. I also now realize that there's real pleasure in working and earning some money, no matter how small an amount." From the tone of her voice I could tell that she was obviously still on a high after her divorce, and, having seen my own mother, I feared that all this excitement and energy would soon dissipate, but, even so, I just nodded. "Well," she said, "I hope you two can learn from your mothers and that you won't have unhappy marriages. Mind you," she continued, "even an unhappy marriage is better than nothing because a divorced woman doesn't get lonely as long as she has a child, so even if you don't get married, you should have a child." Hanako and I looked at each other. "We are now in an age," declared Hanako's mother, with bravado, "when women can do whatever they like."

When Hanako and I returned to our apartment in Mejiro, totally exhausted, we agreed that only a woman with no experience of the world could be naïve enough to claim there was pleasure in working to earn just a small amount of money; but we stayed up late, nevertheless, deciding what we would buy with the money we'd earned from our holiday work.

Afterword

As someone who grew up reading girls' novels, I have long wished to write at least one of these myself, perhaps as a way of saying thank you for all the pleasure I experienced reading these works.

Indian Summer lacks a number of the essential elements of the girls' novel genre and we might therefore hesitate to label it as such. Nevertheless, I think it is true to say that the girl narrator of this novel, whom I almost think of as a family member, lives her life quite courageously and undoubtedly represents certain feelings of the girl of a certain period.

Frankly, I can't help feeling a little uneasy about what the future holds for young women like Momoko and Hanako. Will they fall in love successfully? Will they find a job? Perhaps I am worrying unnecessarily, although I suspect it is natural for an aunt to have these kinds of concerns about a niece.

Afterword to the Paperback Edition

In September or October of 1988 I frankly confessed in the afterword to the hardcover edition of *Indian Summer* to having concerns about what the future held for young women like Momoko and Hanako.

So whatever happened to these girls?

I was so interested in discovering this myself that I am now in the middle of writing the sequel, entitled *Two or Three Things I Know about Her (and Her Friends)*, which tells of Momoko's and Hanako's lives after *Indian Summer*.

Indian Summer is something of a girls' novel. Like the writers of many girls' novels throughout the world, I found that my readers, too, were curious to find out what had happened to the novel's protagonists. This was a factor also in my beginning a sequel. Since there will be some readers who undoubtedly did not meet Momoko and Hanako when they first appeared ten years ago, it gives me great pleasure to introduce them now in paperback form.

May this new edition of *Indian Summer* find many new readers.

February 1999
Kanai Mieko, Author

CORNELL EAST ASIA SERIES

CORNELL
East Asia Series

www.einaudi.cornell.edu/eastasia/publications

www.ingramcontent.com/pod-product-compliance
Lightning Source LLC
Chambersburg PA
CBHW020020030726
47499CB00007B/2200